U0138329

# Anna Karenina

Grade 5

# LET'S ENJOY MASTERPIECES!

This series of **Let's Enjoy Masterpieces** are a special reading comprehension booster program, devised to improve reading comprehension for beginners whose command of English is not satisfactory, or who are elementary, middle, and high school students. With this program, you can enjoy reading masterpieces in English with fun and efficiency.

This carefully planned program is composed of 5 levels, from the beginner level of 350 words to the intermediate and advanced levels of 1,000 words. With this program's level-by-level system, you are able to read famous texts in English and to savor the true pleasure of the world's language.

The program is well conceived, composed of reader-friendly explanations of English expressions and grammar, quizzes to help the student learn vocabulary and understand the meaning of the texts, and fabulous illustrations that adorn every page. In addition, with our "Guide to Listening," not only is reading comprehension enhanced but also listening comprehension skills are highlighted.

In the audio recording of the book, texts are vividly read by professional American actors. The texts are rewritten, according to the levels of the readers by an expert editorial staff of native speakers, on the basis of standard American English with the ministry of education recommended vocabulary. Therefore, it will be of great help even for all the students that want to learn English.

# Introduction

列夫・托爾斯泰

Lev Nikolaevich Tolstoy (1828-1910)

Leo Nikolaevich Tolstoy, or Count Lev Nikolayevich Tolstoy ranks as one of the world's greatest writers and philosophers. Tolstoy was born into a family of aristocratic landowners. He was the fourth child of the family. After he dropped out of university, he returned home. As a landowner, he tried to improve the lives of peasants in his feudal estate. However, after he failed to realize his ideals, he began to live promiscuously, and then in 1851, he joined the army and served in actual military campaigns. During this period, his war experiences influenced him to write a lot of works that provided comprehensive insight into life and death, ethnic issues, and massacres. When he left the army service in 1855, he was already acknowledged as a rising new talent in literature. After his marriage in 1862, he began to concentrate on writing.

His most famous works are *War and Peace, Anna Karenina, and Resurrection*. His writings include common themes of universal love, good and evil, religion and distrust, and the meaning of life and death. Tolstoy used his particular power of persuasion to deal with these themes in an easy-to-understand and interesting manner.

During the 82 years of his life, Tolstoy wrote around 90 works, Tolstoy, along with Dostoevsky, is regarded as one of the giants of Russian literature.

*Anna Karenina* is a novel that describes many of the social problems and customs in Russia in the 1870s. It is one of Tolstoy's masterpieces. This novel has been made into movies many times, and it is a love story about beautiful Anna and Count Vronsky, who is a nobleman and an army officer.

Anna lives a regular married life in St. Petersburg. Then she goes to Moscow to help her brother with his marriage problems. At the Moscow train station, she meets Count Vronsky, who is waiting for his mother. The two of them fall in love. When Anna becomes pregnant with Vronsky's child, he wants her to get divorced and to come live with him, but Anna hesitates because she doesn't want to leave her son.

Anna's husband, Karenin, who is a senior statesman and twenty years older than Anna, hears her confession that she loves Vronsky, yet he refuses to divorce her because of his social position and out of a desire for revenge . . .

# contents

# Before You Read

The characters from *Anna Karenina* are going to introduce themselves.
Please greet them with a warm welcome.

## Anna

I am a wealthy lady from the very upper class[1] in Russian society. Although I have a son, my youthful beauty has not gone away. My husband, Karenin, is an important government official. Sometimes he is very cold, and his love is not passionate[2]. But I never thought that I was unhappy until I traveled to Moscow to visit my brother. I met a man there who changed my life...

## Vronsky

I am a Russian military[3] officer. My family is very wealthy, and my future is very bright. The only thing that would ruin my career and my life is that my love for a beautiful lady is blinded. But even then, I would be an honorable[4] man. Honor is very important to me.

1. upper class 上流社會
2. passionate ['pæʃənɪt] (a.) 熱烈的
3. military ['mɪlɪteri] (a.) 軍事的；軍隊的
4. honorable ['ɑːnərəbəl] (a.) 光榮的
5. stop A from Ving 阻止 A 去做某事
6. beloved [bɪ'lʌvɪd] (a.) 親愛的
7. affair [ə'fer] (n.) 婚外情

# Karenin

I am a very busy government official. My work and my place in society is very important to me. I am married to a beautiful woman. I do love her, and I am sure my wife is happy and would never leave me.

# Stiva

I work for the government, but this is just my job, not my life. Life is too short to waste time on things you do not enjoy. I always have time to enjoy a good meal or a drink with my friends. Women? Yes, I am married, but that does not stop me from meeting[5] others.

# Dolly

Oh, my husband, my beloved[6] Stiva, had an affair[7] with our French nanny! This is terrible! What should I do? Oh, Stiva has invited his sister, Anna, to come and talk to me. That's good. She is so wise in these matters.

# CHAPTER ONE

# An Unhappy Household[1]

**H**appy families are all alike, but unhappy families are unhappy in their own unique[2] ways.

The Oblonsky household was one such unhappy family. Dolly, the wife, had found out three days ago that her husband was having an affair with[3] the French tutor[4]. She announced[5] that she could not go on living in the same house with her husband. She had stayed in her room, and her husband, Prince Stepan Oblonsky, had stayed away from[6] home during the day. Their five

1. household ['haʊshoʊld] (n.) 家庭
2. unique [juːˈniːk] (a.) 獨一無二的
3. have an affair with 有外遇
4. tutor ['tuːtər] (n.) 家庭教師
5. announce [əˈnaʊns] (v.) 宣布；聲稱
6. stay away from 不在家
7. run wild 到處跑
8. servant ['sɜːrvənt] (n.) 僕人
9. quarrel ['kwɔːrəl] (n.) 爭吵；不和
10. leather ['leðər] (a.) 皮製的
11. couch [kaʊtʃ] (n.) 長沙發
12. reach up for 伸手拿到
13. robe [roʊb] (n.) 長袍
14. vanish ['vænɪʃ] (v.) 消失

children ran wild[7] around the house. The cook quit, and the other servants[8] were thinking of doing the same.

On the third morning after the quarrel[9], Prince Oblonsky, who was called Stiva by his friends, woke up on the leather[10] couch[11] in his study. He had just had a wonderful dream, and he was smiling as he reached up for[12] his robe[13]. Suddenly, he realized that he was in his study and his robe was in his wife's bedroom. The smile on his face vanished[14].

"It's all my fault," Stiva thought. "Dolly will never forgive[1] me! What have I done? But the real tragedy[2] is that I cannot really be blamed[3]!"

Stiva remembered how he had come home from the theater three nights ago. He had found his wife in their upstairs[4] bedroom with a letter from the French tutor in her hand. The memory[5] of the look of pain on his wife's face and the tears in her eyes still stabbed[6] his heart.

The affair with the French tutor was not the first for Stiva. He was thirty-four years old and was quite handsome and charming[7]. Women younger than his wife were constantly[8] attracted to[9] him. The biggest problem was that he was no longer in love with his wife. She was a good wife and mother, but she was no longer a beautiful young woman.

---

1. forgive [fərˈgɪv] (v.) 原諒
2. tragedy [ˈtrædʒədi] (n.) 悲劇
3. blame [bleɪm] (v.) 責備;指責
4. upstairs [ʌpˈsterz] (a.) 樓上的
5. memory [ˈmeməri] (n.) 記憶;紀念
6. stab [stæb] (v.) 刺;刺傷
7. charming [ˈtʃɑːrmɪŋ] (a.) 迷人的
8. constantly [ˈkɑːnstəntli] (adv.) 一直
9. be attracted to 被⋯⋯吸引
10. telegram [ˈtelɪgræm] (n.) 電報
11. brighten [ˈbraɪtn] (v.) 變明亮
12. content [ˈkɑːntent] (n.) 內容
13. current [ˈkɜːrənt] (a.) 當前的
14. situation [ˌsɪtʃuˈeɪʃən] (n.) 情況;處境

Stiva rang the
bell for his servant,
who came in with a
telegram[10]. Stiva opened
it, and his face quickly
brightened[11] when he
read the contents[12].
His sister, Anna, was
coming for a visit.

Anna lived in St. Petersburg with her husband
and eight-year-old son. Dolly really liked Anna.
Stiva had invited his sister to visit and try to
solve the current[13] situation[14]. The telegram said
that Anna would arrive in Moscow by train later
today.

---

**One Point**

Stiva rang the bell for his servant, **who** came in with a telegram.
史帝沃按鈴叫了僕人，僕人拿了一封電報走進來。

---

**形容詞子句**：包含在主要句子之下，有主詞和動詞的完整說明句。上句中
who 所引導的子句用來說明主要句子的 his servant。
*ex.* He is an old, rich man, **who** has two sons.
　　他是位老而富有的男人，膝下有二子。

Stiva dressed and then opened the door from his study to his wife's bedroom. Dolly was standing in front of an open wardrobe[1]. She was trying to decide if she should pack[2] her things[3] and leave with the children. In spite of her anger, Stiva was her husband, and in her heart, Dolly still loved him.

"Anna is coming today," said Stiva in a soft voice.

1. wardrobe [ˈwɔːrdroʊb] (n.)
   衣櫃；衣櫥
2. pack [pæk] (v.) 收拾
3. thing [θɪŋ] (n.) 東西
4. exclaim [ɪkˈskleɪm] (v.) 呼喊；驚叫
5. mistress [ˈmɪstrɪs] (n.) 情婦
6. repulsive [rɪˈpʌlsɪv] (a.) 令人反感的
7. scream [skriːm] (v.) 尖叫
8. slam [slæm] (v.) 猛地關上
9. downstairs [daʊnˈsterz] (adv.) 樓下
10. leave for 動身前往
11. courthouse [ˈkɔːrthaʊs] (n.)
    縣府大樓

"Well, what is that to me? I can't see her!" exclaimed[4] Dolly. "I am going to take the children and leave this house. You can live here with your mistress[5]!"

"Dolly, please understand. . ." said Stiva.

"Understand? You are a repulsive[6], hateful man!"

"Dolly, please think of the children. It would ruin them to grow up without their father. Don't punish them. Punish me! I'm the guilty one," Stiva pleaded.

Without a word, Dolly stood and moved toward the door.

"Dolly, one more word," Stiva said, as Dolly opened the door.

"Go away!" screamed[7] Dolly, and she slammed[8] the door closed behind her.

Sadly, Stiva went downstairs[9] and told his servant to prepare a room for Anna. Then he left for[10] his office at one of Moscow's courthouses[11].

### Check Up

Which words best describe Dolly's state of mind?

a  Clear and decided

b  Unsure and in turmoil

c  Serene and calm

Ans: b

As a student, Stiva was intelligent[1], but he had been lazy and mischievous[2]. However, most of the rich and powerful in Russia knew his father, and these connections[3] helped him get a high-paying job in the government. Stiva was not a man who had great ambitions, and he did not work hard. He relied on[4] his charming manners and quick wits[5] to make people happy.

At noon, Stiva was leaving a meeting when he saw a broad-shouldered[6] man running lightly[7] up the stairs toward him. Stiva smiled in pleasure.

"Levin, what a pleasant surprise! What are you doing in Moscow?" said Stiva.

"I must ask you something," said Levin. Suddenly, he seemed to[8] be shy. "Would you happen to know what the Shcherbatskys are doing?"

1. intelligent [ɪnˈtelɪdʒənt]
   (a.) 有才智的
2. mischievous [ˈmɪstʃɪvəs]
   (a.) 調皮的
3. connection [kəˈnekʃən] (n.) 關係
4. rely on 依靠
5. wit [wɪt] (n.) 機智；風趣
6. broad-shouldered
   [ˈbrɔːdˈʃouldərd] (a.) 強壯的
7. lightly [ˈlaɪtli] (adv.) 慢慢地
8. seem to 似乎；好像
9. immediately [ɪˈmiːdiətli] (n.) 立即
10. in the meantime 同時

Stiva immediately[9] knew why Levin had come back to Moscow. It was no secret to him that Levin was in love with Princess Kitty Shcherbatsky, Dolly's younger sister.

"The Shcherbatskys are having a dinner party tonight at eight o'clock," replied Stiva with a smile. "I will send over a servant to announce your arrival in Moscow. Of course, you will be invited. Kitty will be there. In the meantime[10], let's go get lunch."

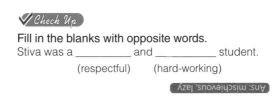

Fill in the blanks with opposite words.
Stiva was a _____ and _____ student.
(respectful)    (hard-working)

Ans: mischievous, lazy

17

Over lunch, Stiva asked, "So why did you stay away from Moscow for so long? And why have you suddenly returned?"

"As you have guessed, I am in love with Kitty," replied Levin. "I left Moscow because I thought she would not agree to[1] marry[2] me. Her mother especially[3] doesn't seem to like me. But I couldn't stop[4] thinking about her." Levin sighed[5]. Then he burst out[6], "I've come back to ask Kitty to[7] marry me. Do you think there's any possibility[8] she will say 'yes'?"

1. agree to 同意；接受
2. marry ['mæri] (v.) 結婚
3. especially [ɪ'speʃəli] (adv.) 尤其是
4. stop [stɑːp] (v.) 停止
5. sigh [saɪ] (v.) 嘆氣
6. burst out 大聲説出
7. ask A to 要求 A 去

8. possibility [ˌpɑːsə'bɪləti] (adv.) 可能性
9. relieved [rɪ'liːvd] (a.) 放心的
10. rival ['raɪvəl] (n.) 競爭者
11. cavalry ['kævəlri] (n.) 裝甲兵
12. officer ['ɔːfɪsər] (n.) 官員

"Of course," said Stiva. "Dolly told me that she thinks Kitty loves you."

"That's wonderful!" cried Levin, who looked both relieved[9] and surprised.

"There's just one thing you must know," said Stiva. "You have a rival[10]. His name is Count Vronsky. He's a young cavalry[11] officer[12] with many powerful connections. Kitty's mother really likes him, but I am sure that Kitty loves you more. Go to the dinner party early before Vronsky arrives, and ask her to marry you. Good luck!"

Stiva went off to meet Anna at the train station, while Levin went back to his apartment.

✔ *Check Up*  True or False.

ⓐ Levin thinks Kitty's mother approves of him.  _____

ⓑ Vronsky is a nobody in Russian social circles.  _____

Ans: a. F  b. F

## St. Petersburg:
# The Jewel of Russia

In Anna Karenina's time, St. Petersburg was the capital of Russia. It was the most important and most beautiful of all Russian cities in the 19th century. Peter the Great founded[1] the city in 1704 as a "gateway to Europe". The city is situated[2] on the coast of the Gulf of Finland, which provides easy access by ship to the countries of northern Europe. Peter the Great and his allies[3] built huge palaces, which still stand today, for themselves. Ornate[4] and beautiful churches were built here and there among the houses and government buildings.

1. found [faʊnd] (v.) 建立
2. be situated 位於
3. ally [əˈlaɪ] (n.) 同盟者
4. ornate [ɔːrˈneɪt] (a.) 富麗的
5. granite [ˈɡrænɪt] (n.) 花崗岩
6. embankment [ɪmˈbæŋkmənt] (n.) 堤岸
7. canal [kəˈnæl] (n.) 運河
8. permanent [ˈpɜːrmənənt] (a.) 永久的
9. appropriate [əˈproʊpriət] (a.) 適當的

Peter the Great was inspired by the cities of Amsterdam and Venice, when he decided to build granite[5] embankments[6] to contain the waters of the Neva River which now flows through the city through many canals[7]. Peter the Great imagined that the citizens could get around by boat and forbade the construction of any permanent[8] bridges, and none were built until 1850.

The city became the jewel of Russia, and Anna, Tolstoy's heroine, became the jewel of St. Petersburg. It is appropriate[9] that Anna be cast as living in St. Petersburg. Her husband, the ambitious high government official would of course pursue his career in the Russia's capital city. Also, St. Petersburg is the

home to the finest in Russian society – with all the operas, balls, and high society of Russia. No other city would be quite as perfect as St. Petersburg for the setting of *Anna Karenina.*

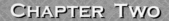

# CHAPTER TWO

## A Chance Meeting[1]

**A**t the train station, Oblonsky met Count Vronsky while waiting for the train from St. Petersburg.

"Who are you meeting?" asked Vronsky.

"I've come to meet a pretty woman," replied Stiva. "My sister, Anna."

"Oh, Karenin's wife?" said Vronsky.

"Yes. So you know her?"

"No, not really. . . I don't remember," said Vronsky.

The name Karenin gave him the impression[2] of someone very official[3] and boring.

"But you must know my respected[4] brother-in-law[5]. He's a high government official," said Stiva.

---

1. chance meeting 邂逅
2. impression [ɪmˈprɛʃən] (n.) 印象
3. official [əˈfɪʃəl] (a.) 官方的
4. respected [rɪˈspɛktɪd] (n.) 受尊敬的
5. brother-in-law 小叔
6. by sight 見過面
7. religious [rɪˈlɪdʒəs] (a.) 虔誠的
8. interrupt [ˌɪntəˈrʌpt] (v.) 打斷講話

"Yes," replied Vronsky. "I know him by reputation and by sight[6]. I know that he's quite clever and religious[7]. Anyway, I am here to welcome my mother."

Their conversation was interrupted[8] by the sound of the train approaching[9]. When it came to a stop[10], a young guard jumped off near Vronsky. Vronsky asked the guard which carriage the Countess Vronsky was in. The guard pointed, and Vronsky went to the carriage[11] door. Just as he reached it, he stepped aside[12] for a lady getting out[13].

9. approach [ə'proutʃ] (v.) 接近
10. come to a stop 停止
11. carriage ['kærɪdʒ] (n.) 車廂

12. step aside 讓開
13. get out 出來

At a glance[1], Vronsky knew that the lady was
very wealthy[2]. He looked closely at her lovely face
because he thought he had seen something special
there. As he did, she also looked at him and gave
him a friendly, curious[3] look.

Vronsky nodded[4] and then climbed the steps
into the carriage. His mother, an old lady with
black eyes and curls[5], smiled at him with her thin
lips.

1. at a glance 一瞥
2. wealthy ['welθi] (a.) 富有的
3. curious ['kjʊriəs] (a.) 不尋常的
4. nod [nɑːd] (v.) 點頭表示
5. curl [kɜːrl] (n.) 捲髮

6. journey ['dʒɜːrni] (n.) 旅行
7. confused [kənˈfjuːzd] (a.) 迷惑的
8. crowd [kraʊd] (n.) 人群；一堆
9. call over 叫某人過來

"So you got my telegram," she said. "Are you well?"

"Did you have a good journey[6]?" asked Vronsky as he sat down beside her. Just then, the lady Vronsky had seen leaving came back into the carriage, looking confused[7].

"Have you found your brother?" asked Countess Vronsky.

Suddenly, Vronsky knew that this was Anna Karenina, Oblonsky's sister.

"Your brother is just outside," said Vronsky. "Please wait here, and I will call him."

Anna smiled and sat next to the Countess. Vronsky left the train and saw Oblonsky through the crowd[8]. He called him over[9] and said, "Your sister is sitting next to my mother in this carriage."

---

✅ Check Up

The first meeting between Vronsky and Anna was one of _____.

a curiosity
b love at first sight
c indifference

Ans: a

As soon as Anna saw her brother from the window, she came out of the carriage and ran to him. She threw her arms around[1] him and kissed his cheeks warmly. Vronsky helped his mother down the carriage steps.

"She's quite charming, isn't she?" said the Countess to her son. Then to Anna, she said, "I can speak plainly[2] at my age. I must confess[3] I have lost my heart to[4] you."

Anna looked delighted. She kissed the Countess and then offered her hand to Vronsky. He kissed it and felt a great joy.

Just then, there was a great commotion[5], as the stationmaster[6] and several conductors[7] ran past. Their faces were pale and frightened[8]. Vronsky suggested the women go back into the carriage. Then he and Stiva followed the train officials to the front of the train. It was clear that something terrible had happened.

1. throw one's arms around 用雙手擁抱
2. plainly ['pleɪnli] (adv.) 明顯地
3. confess [kənˈfɛs] (v.) 坦白
4. lose one's heart to 十分喜愛
5. commotion [kəˈmoʊʃən] (n.) 騷動
6. stationmaster ['steɪʃənˌmæstər] (n.) 站長
7. conductor [kənˈdʌktər] (n.) 指揮；車掌
8. frightened ['fraɪtnd] (a.) 驚嚇的
9. be crushed to death 被輾死
10. be about to 即將要

A guard had been crushed to death[9] under the train as it had arrived. At the sight of his dead body, Stiva looked very upset, as if he were about to[10] cry.

"Oh, this is terrible!" he exclaimed.

There was nothing Vronsky or Stiva could do, so they returned to the carriage where Anna and the Countess were waiting.

**One Point**

Vronsky **suggested** the woman go back into the carriage.
馮斯基建議女士們先回到車廂。

----

**suggest + that**：某人要求另一人做某事。句型為 A + suggest that + B should…。that 中的子句要用原形動詞表示其重要性，should 可省略。suggest、demand、insist 等動詞都屬於這種用法。
*ex.* She **insisted** that we (should) stay one more night.
　　她堅持要我們多留一天。

"It was terrible," said Stiva, as he told Anna and the Countess what had happened. "And his poor widow[1] was there. She threw herself on his body and said she had a large family. What an awful[2] thing!"

"Isn't there anything anyone can do?" asked Anna, her eyes filling with[3] tears.

Vronsky looked at her and immediately left the carriage. When he returned a few minutes later, Stiva was telling the ladies about the latest[4]

1. widow ['wɪdoʊ] (n.) 寡婦
2. awful ['ɔːfəl] (a.) 可怕的
3. fill with 充滿
4. the latest 最新的

5. address [ə'dres] (v.) 向某人說話
6. a large sum of 一大筆
7. respective [rɪ'spektɪv] (a.) 各自的
8. mood [muːd] (n.) 心情；情緒

play in Moscow. They left the carriage together and walked toward the exit. As they reached the doors, the stationmaster came running up behind them.

Addressing[5] Count Vronsky, he said, "You gave my assistant a large sum of[6] money, sir. What did you want us to do with it?"

"Well, it's for the widow and her children, of course," replied Vronsky.

"You gave money?" asked Stiva. "Very kind! Very kind!"

Each couple took a separate carriage from the station to their respective[7] houses. On the carriage ride home, Anna asked, "Have you known Vronsky long?"

"Yes. You know, he's hoping to marry Kitty."

At this news, Anna's mood[8] changed.

"Really?" she said softly. "Now let's talk about your affairs."

✓ Check Up

**Why did Vronsky give money to the stationmaster's assistant?**

a  Because he wanted them to improve the station.

b  Because Anna felt sad for the dead man's family.

c  Because he felt guilty about the man's death.

Ans:b

Stiva told Anna everything. When they arrived at his house, he dropped her off[1] and drove back[2] to his office at the courthouse.

Although Dolly had told Stiva she did not care if Anna came or not, she was relieved to see her.

"After all[3], it's not Anna's fault," she told herself. "I only know her as a dear friend."

When Anna came in, Dolly greeted[4] her eagerly[5] and kissed her.

"Dolly, I'm so glad to see you!" said Anna.

Anna listened very sympathetically[6] to Dolly, and Dolly felt much better after telling the story of her troubles.

"Oh, what shall I do, Anna?" asked Dolly when she had finished. "Please help me."

"Dolly, Stiva is still in love with you," said Anna.

1. drop off 放下
2. drive back 趕回去
3. after all 畢竟
4. greet [griːt] (v.) 迎接
5. eagerly [ˈiːɡərli] (adv.) 熱切地
6. sympathetically [ˌsɪmpəˈθetɪkli] (adv.) 悲憐地
7. betray [bɪˈtreɪ] (v.) 背叛
8. for a moment 一會兒

"I am his sister, and I can read his heart. He wasn't in love with the other woman – he didn't betray[7] you in his heart."

"But what if it happens again?" asked Dolly. "Would you forgive him?"

"I don't think it will happen again," replied Anna. Then she thought for a moment[8]. "Yes, I would forgive him."

**One Point**

But **what if** it happens again?
萬一事情再次發生怎麼辦？

- - - - - - - - - - - - - - - - - - - - - - - - - - - - - - - - - - - - - - - - - - -

**what if ?**：表示「萬一⋯⋯如何」或是「要是⋯⋯怎麼辦」
*ex.* **What if** he refuses it? 萬一他拒絕了怎麼辦？

In the end[1], Anna persuaded Dolly to[2] forgive
Stiva. Just after Dolly agreed to forgive her
husband, Kitty arrived. She had come over to
see her older sister Dolly.

Kitty had never formally met Anna, but she
knew who she was. Kitty hoped this fashionable[3]
woman from St. Petersburg would not think

1. in the end 最後
2. persuade A to 說服 A 去
3. fashionable ['fæʃnəbl] (a.)
   流行的；時髦的
4. get along 相處
5. chat [tʃæt] (v.) 聊天；閒談

6. grand [grænd] (a.) 重大的
7. ball [bɔːl] (n.) 舞會
8. blush [blʌʃ] (v.) 臉紅
9. generous ['dʒenərəs] (a.)
   寬宏大量的
10. be grateful to 感激

she was a silly young girl. Anna did like Kitty, and they both got along[4] well. All three of them chatted[5] for about an hour.

Before Kitty left, she told Anna, "Oh, you must come to the grand[6] ball[7] next week. Many important and fashionable people will be there!"

"And your Count Vronsky?" asked Anna.

Kitty blushed[8].

"I had the pleasure of meeting him at the train station today," said Anna. "He seems to be a very handsome and generous[9] man. I think I will stay for the grand ball next week."

Kitty left, and Dolly told the servants to prepare dinner. That night, Dolly, Stiva, Anna, and all the children had dinner together. Dolly also called her husband "Stiva", which she had not done for three days. This pleased Stiva very much, and he was grateful to[10] Anna.

Across town, the Shcherbatskys' butler[1] announced Levin's arrival at seven thirty. When Kitty heard this, she felt excited but was also afraid. She knew why he had come early.

Levin entered the hall and found Kitty standing there alone. He looked at her with excitement, but he was also shy.

"My dear, Levin! I heard you had returned to Moscow!" exclaimed Kitty. "How long will you stay this time?"

"Well, that depends on[2] you," he said. "I mean, what you should understand is, I came to . . . be my wife!"

Kitty felt overjoyed[3], which surprised her. She was very fond of[4] Levin, whom she had known since childhood. However, she thought of Levin more like a brother than a possible husband. She did not expect to[5] feel such strong emotions at his marriage proposal[6]. But then she remembered Vronsky, and she looked at Levin steadily[7].

---

1. butler ['bʌtlər] (n.) 男管家
2. depend on 取決於
3. overjoyed [,ouvər'dʒɔɪd] (a.) 欣喜若狂
4. be fond of 喜歡
5. expect to 期望
6. proposal [prə'pouzəl] (n.) 求婚
7. steadily ['stedəli] (adv.) 鎮靜地
8. stand still 站著不動

"No, it cannot be," she said softly. "Forgive me."

Levin stood still[8] for a moment. Then he said with a broken heart, "No, of course you can't. I understand."

Levin was about to leave, when a handsome man in a uniform came in. Levin watched Kitty greet Vronsky. Her eyes and face were bright as she looked at him. He could see that Kitty truly loved Vronsky.

✓ Check Up

**Fill in the blank.**
How long Levin stays in Moscow _____ on Kitty.

Ans: depends

35

The next week, the grand ball was being held[1] at a large palace[2] in Moscow. As the guests began to arrive, the sounds of their voices and laughter filled the rooms and halls. Kitty and her mother arrived fashionably late. Kitty was the perfect image of beauty in her black dress. Many

1. be held 被舉行
2. palace ['pæləs] (n.) 豪華住宅
3. admiringly [əd'maɪərɪŋli] (adv.) 讚美地
4. ballroom ['bɔːlruːm] (n.) 舞廳
5. at once 立即
6. beat [biːt] (n.) 跳動
7. uniformed ['juːnɪfɔːrmd] (a.) 穿制服的
8. compliment ['kɑːmplɪmənt] (v.) 恭維
9. appearance [ə'pɪrəns] (n.) 外貌
10. propose marriage to 求婚

people looked at her admiringly[3] as she walked up the steps with her mother to the grand ballroom[4].

At once[5], Kitty saw that the most important people at the ball were talking together in one corner of the room. Stiva was there with Dolly. Anna, in a beautiful black velvet dress, was also there. She did not look like a woman who had an eight-year-old son. He was also there − Kitty's love, Count Vronsky. Kitty's heart beat[6] a little faster at the sight of the uniformed[7] Count.

As Kitty joined the group, Anna smiled at her and complimented[8] her dress and beautiful appearance[9]. Count Vronksy asked Kitty to dance. While they danced, they did not talk about anything important, but Kitty was not worried. She was sure that he would ask her to dance the most important dance of the evening: the mazurka. Kitty was sure that Count Vronsky would propose marriage to[10] her at that time.

After this first dance, Kitty had to dance with several young men who were competing[1] to dance with her. She could not refuse[2] them. As she danced with one of these young men, she suddenly saw Anna dancing with Count Vronsky next to her. Kitty became slightly[3] alarmed[4], and she watched Anna and Vronsky closely. Anna was looking up at the Count with bright eyes. Every time he spoke to her, she seemed to be filled with joy, and her eyes became brighter. To Kitty's horror, the same expression[5] of excitement and happiness was reflected[6] on Vronsky's face.

When the mazurka finally began, Kitty was asked to dance by an old family friend, Korunsky. She accepted, as she could see Vronsky was already dancing with Anna. The more Kitty looked at them, the more she realized that they were very attracted to each other. Kitty was heartbroken[7].

1. compete [kəm'piːt] (v.) 競爭
2. refuse [rɪ'fjuːz] (v.) 拒絕
3. slightly ['slaɪtli] (adv.) 稍微
4. alarmed [ə'lɑːrmd] (a.) 擔心的
5. expression [ɪk'spreʃən] (n.) 表情
6. reflect [rɪ'flekt] (v.) 反映
7. heartbroken ['hɑːrt,broʊkən] (a.) 心碎的
8. move away 移走
9. despair [dɪ'sper] (n.) 絕望
10. jealousy ['dʒeləsi] (n.) 妒忌

Later in the dance, Anna and Kitty found
themselves dancing next to each other. Anna
reached out her hand to Kitty, but Kitty ignored it
and moved away[8]. Suddenly, Anna saw the look
of despair[9] and jealousy[10] on Kitty's face.

*Check Up* True or False.

[a] At the dance, Kitty was expected to dance with many young men. ____
[b] Kitty became jealous of Anna and Vronsky during the dance. ____

Ans: a. T b. T

39

After the dance, Anna told Vronsky she would not stay for dinner.

"Thank you for the wonderful time," she said.

"Now I must go home and prepare for my journey back home tomorrow."

"So you really are leaving tomorrow?" asked Vronsky.

"Yes, I must," replied Anna.

Her eyes shone[1], and her smile warmed Vronsky's heart.

Early the next morning, Anna sent a telegram to her husband telling him she would leave today for St. Petersburg on the overnight[2] train.

"I must go," she told Dolly. "And I must confess the reason for my sudden[3] departure[4]. I have ruined it for Kitty and Vronsky. She's jealous of[5] me, and I made the ball last night torture[6] for her. But it's really not my fault — or at least, just a little bit[7]."

---

1. shine [ʃaɪn] (v.) 照耀
2. overnight [ˌoʊvərˈnaɪt] (a.) 晚上的
3. sudden [ˈsʌdn] (a.) 突然的；意外的
4. departure [dɪˈpɑːrtʃər] (n.) 離開
5. be jealous of 妒忌
6. torture [ˈtɔːrtʃər] (n.) 折磨；痛苦
7. a little bit 有點
8. sound like 聽起來

"You sound like[8] my Stiva!" exclaimed Dolly. "But remember, Anna, I'll always love you as my dearest friend. I won't forget what you did for me!"

That night, as Anna rode on the train home, she felt relieved and happy to be going home.

"Soon I will see my son Seriozha and my husband," she said to herself. "Then my simple life will continue as before."

✔️ *Check Up*

Who does Dolly compare Anna to?

a Kitty

b Anna's husband

c Dolly's husband

Ans: c

Comprehension Quiz

## A Match.

❶ Anna Karenina ·              · ⓐ A very handsome military officer

❷ Count Vronsky ·              · ⓑ A married woman who falls in love with another man

❸ Kitty ·              · ⓒ A mother who does not feel loved by her husband

❹ Dolly ·              · ⓓ A young and beautiful princess whom Levin loves

## B Fill in the blanks with the given words.

> got along    decide if    think of    relied on    stay away

❶ Dolly was trying to _____ she should leave or stay.

❷ Stiva begged Dolly to _____ the children.

❸ Anna liked Kitty, and they _____ well.

❹ "Why did you _____ from Moscow for so long?" asked Stiva.

❺ Stiva _____ his charm to be successful in business.

## C Choose the correct answer.

❶ Why was Dolly upset with her husband Stiva?

(a) Because he wrote a love letter to Dolly's sister Kitty.

(b) Because she discovered he was having an affair with the French tutor.

(c) Because he told her he did not love her any more.

❷ Why was Kitty horrified at the ball?

(a) Because her mother wanted her to marry Levin.

(b) Because Levin fell in love with Anna.

(c) Because she saw how Vronsky behaved toward Anna.

❸ What did Kitty do when Levin asked her to marry him?

(a) She refused his proposal.

(b) She accepted his proposal.

(c) She stood still and said nothing.

## D Rearrange the sentences in chronological order.

❶ A man is crushed to death by the train.

❷ Levin proposes to Kitty.

❸ Vronsky gives money to the stationmaster.

❹ Vronsky dances with Anna at the ball.

❺ Oblonsky meets Vronsky at the train station.

# CHAPTER THREE

_____ ⇨ _____ ⇨ _____ ⇨ _____ ⇨ _____

# Romance in St. Petersburg

There was a terrible snowstorm outside. Anna tried to read a novel, but she could not concentrate[1]. She listened to the sound of the train and fell asleep. Suddenly, she realized that the train was coming to a stop on the way to St. Petersburg. After a while[2], a man in a military[3] overcoat[4] approached her.

"May I assist[5] you, lady?" he said.

Anna recognized[6] Vronsky as he spoke.

"I didn't know you were coming to St. Petersburg!" exclaimed Anna joyously. "What business do you have there?"

---

1. concentrate ['kɑːnsəntreɪt]
(v.) 集中
2. after a while 過了一會兒
3. military ['mɪləteri] (a.) 軍隊的
4. overcoat ['oʊvərkoʊt] (n.)
外套；大衣
5. assist [ə'sɪst] (v.) 協助
6. recognize ['rekəgnaɪz] (v.) 認出

7. torn [tɔːrn] (a.) 掙扎的
8. beg [beg] (v.) 懇求
9. familiar [fə'mɪljər] (a.) 熟悉的
10. dissatisfaction
[dɪˌsætɪs'fækʃən] (n.) 不悅
11. arise [ə'raɪz] (v.) 產生
12. passion ['pæʃən] (n.) 熱情

"Can you not guess?" asked Vronsky. "I have come to be where you are."

Anna felt torn[7] between joy and fear. For a long time, she was silent. Then she said, "You should not say that, and I beg[8] you, if you are a gentleman, to forget it, as I shall forget it." With that, she closed her eyes and tried to sleep.

Early the next morning, Alexey Alexandrovitch Karenin was waiting for his wife on the train platform. He saw Anna as soon as she stepped from her carriage. Anna also saw her husband immediately. The familiar[9] feeling of dissatisfaction[10] upon seeing her husband arose[11] in Anna. To Anna, her husband was cold, without feeling or passion[12].

Vronsky stepped down[1] from the train and saw Karenin take hold of[2] his wife's arm as if she were a piece of property[3]. For the first time[4], Vronsky came face to face with the fact that there was a man attached to[5] Anna. He, too, felt a disagreeable sensation[6] when he saw Karenin. Vronsky approached the couple slowly and said, "Did you have a good night?"

1. step down 走下
2. take hold of 抓住
3. property ['prɑ:pərti] (n.) 財產
4. for the first time 第一次
5. attached to 附屬於
6. sensation [sen'seɪʃən] (n.) 感覺
7. light up 放光彩
8. interruption [ˌɪntə'rʌpʃən] (n.) 打擾
9. make one's acquaintance 結識
10. delighted [dɪ'laɪtɪd] (a.) 愉快的

"Yes, thank you," replied Anna. Her eyes lit up[7] when she spoke to him. Anna looked at her husband to see if he knew Vronsky. Karenin had an unpleasant look on his face. He disliked the interruption[8], and he was trying to remember Vronsky's face.

"This is Count Vronsky," said Anna. "I made his acquaintance[9] in Moscow."

"Ah, we have met before," said Karenin without feeling.

"I hope I may visit you," said Vronsky, more to Anna than Karenin.

"We'd be delighted[10]," said Karenin in a cold voice. "You may find us home on Mondays."

Then he turned, and still holding Anna's arm, they left the station.

 Check Up

**Fill in the blank.**

Another way of saying you met someone is to say that you made that person's _____ .

Ans: acquaintance

When Anna and her husband arrived home, Seriozha, their son, was very happy to see his mother. Anna told him about her visit to Moscow and gave him some presents.

In St. Petersburg, Anna attended[1] operas, balls, and dinner parties with the rich and powerful in Russian society. Count Vronsky's family was one of the richest in Russia, and he also showed up[2] at many of the same events as Anna. He was the commander[3] of an army[4] regiment[5], and he moved his men to St. Petersburg.

Upon her arrival in St. Petersburg, Anna had tried to forget her attraction[6] to Vronsky. However, every time she met him at a dinner party or ball, she was excited and happy to see him. Soon, she realized that Vronsky was the main interest in her life.

1. attend [əˈtɛnd] (v.) 出席
2. show up 露面
3. commander [kəˈmændər] (n.) 指揮官
4. army [ˈɑːrmi] (n.) 陸軍
5. regiment [ˈrɛdʒɪmənt] (n.) 軍團
6. attraction [əˈtrækʃən] (n.) 吸引力
7. outing [ˈaʊtɪŋ] (n.) 短途旅遊
8. escort [ˈɛskɔːt] (v.) 護送；陪同
9. subject [ˈsʌbdʒɪkt] (n.) 主題
10. gossip [ˈgɑːsɪp] (v.) 八卦
11. circle [ˈsɜːrkəl] (n.) 圈子
12. bold [boʊld] (a.) 魯莽的
13. deal with 處理

Anna and Vronsky became very good friends and did many things together. Even when Karenin was too busy to go to the theater or other outings[7], Vronsky would escort[8] Anna. In this way, Anna and Vronsky became lovers. They also became the subject[9] of much gossip[10] among the highest circles[11] of Russian society. Karenin noticed his wife's behavior. He was very worried about what other people might think of him. However, he was not a bold[12] man, so he decided the best way for him to deal with[13] the situation was to ignore it.

One day, Vronsky called on[1] Anna when Karenin was away. He found her on the back porch[2] of her house. Her lovely face looked red and hot.

"What's the matter?" asked Vronsky. "Are you ill?"

"No," said Anna. "I'm pregnant[3]. It's your child."

1. call on 拜訪
2. back porch 後陽台
3. pregnant ['prɛgnənt] (a.) 懷孕的
4. railing ['reɪlɪŋ] (n.) 欄杆
5. put an end to 結束

6. secrecy ['siːkrəsi] (n.) 秘密
7. allow A to 允許 A 去
8. disgrace [dɪs'greɪs] (v.) 使名譽掃地
9. run away 逃跑
10. solution [sə'luːʃən] (n.) 解決辦法

Vronsky turned pale and held the porch railing[4].

"We must put an end to[5] our secrecy[6]. Ask your husband for a divorce, and we will get married." he said.

"He would never agree to that," replied Anna. "He will not allow me to[7] disgrace[8] his family name."

"We have to tell him," said Vronsky. "We cannot continue like this."

"And then what would we do?" asked Anna. "Run away[9]?"

Vronsky thought for a moment. "Yes, that is the only solution[10] then. If he doesn't give you a divorce, we will leave Russia."

Vronsky did not know that this would be very difficult for Anna. She loved Vronsky, but she did not want to be away from her son. However, there was no choice for her.

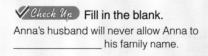

**Check Up** Fill in the blank.
Anna's husband will never allow Anna to
_____ his family name.

Ans: disgrace

When Anna told her husband she loved Vronsky, Karenin was horrified[1]. Until now, he had tried to ignore his wife's relationship with Vronsky. Anna's direct[2] announcement[3] of her love for Vronsky and the fact that she was going to have his child forced him to confront[4] the situation.

Karenin sent his wife to their summer house outside Moscow. He told her he needed time to think.

After much thought[5] in his calculating[6] way, Karenin decided that he should force Anna to remain with him.

"I must not be unhappy, but also Anna should not be happy," he thought. "This is the best solution. I am not getting rid of[7] a guilty wife but am giving her a chance to mend her ways[8]."

---

1. horrified ['hɔːrɪfaɪd] (a.) 驚嚇的
2. direct [dɪ'rɛkt] (a.) 直接的
3. announcement [ə'naʊnsmənt] (n.) 宣布
4. confront [kən'frʌnt] (v.) 面臨
5. thought [θɔːt] (n.) 思考
6. calculating ['kælkjuleɪtɪŋ] (a.) 精明的
7. get rid of 擺脱
8. mend one's way 改正錯誤

He quickly wrote a letter to Anna.

> *Whatever your behavior has been, I do not think that I have the right[9] to cut the bonds[10] that God has made between us. The family cannot be broken because of the sin[11] of one of the partners. Our life must continue as before. I am sure you regret[12] your behavior and will not continue with it. If you do, I am sure you can imagine what the future will hold for you and your son. I ask you to return to our home in St. Petersburg as soon as possible.*
>
> *Karenin*

9. right [raɪt] (n.) 權利
10. bond [bɑːnd] (n.) 聯結
11. sin [sɪn] (n.) 罪
12. regret [rɪˈɡret] (v.) 後悔

Anna returned home as her husband had instructed[1]. She felt helpless[2] in her current situation.

"My life was miserable[3] before," thought Anna. "What will it be like now that[4] Karenin knows I was unfaithful[5]? And what about the baby?"

Anna and her husband lived in the same house, and they met every day for dinner so that the servants would not gossip. However, Anna continued to see Vronsky away from the house. Karenin knew this. He only told Anna that Vronsky was not welcome at the house.

One day, Vronsky received a note from Anna.

> *I feel sick and unhappy. I cannot leave the house, but I want to see you very much. Come by before ten. My husband will be busy in a meeting until then.*

---

1. instruct [ɪnˈstrʌkt] (v.) 指示；吩咐
2. helpless [ˈhɛlpləs] (a.) 無助的
3. miserable [ˈmɪzərəbəl] (a.) 痛苦的；不幸的
4. now that 既然

5. unfaithful [ʌnˈfeɪθfəl] (a.) 不忠的
6. lie down 躺下
7. take a nap 午睡
8. bend over 彎腰
9. frighten [ˈfraɪtn] (v.) 驚嚇

Vronsky was tired, so he lay down[6] to take a nap[7]. He had a strange dream about a dirty old peasant who was bending over[8] and talking to himself in French. This dream frightened[9] Vronksy, but when he woke up he thought that he was being very silly. Then he looked at his watch and saw that it was eight o'clock. He would have to hurry to meet Anna before her husband came back home.

✓ *Check Up*  **True or False.**

[a] Anna and Karenin lived in different houses and ate separately. ____

[b] Vronsky had a strange dream about an old peasant. ____

Ans: a. F  b. T

When Vronsky knocked on[1] Anna's front
door, the servant opened it and gave him a
surprised look. Then it was Vronsky's turn to be
surprised as Karenin appeared. Karenin stopped
and looked at Vronsky with a stern[2] look of
disapproval[3]. Then he stepped outside and
made his way to[4] a waiting carriage, acting as if
Vronsky were not there.

"If he fought me, I could do something,"
thought Vronsky. "But he makes me feel like a
snake in the grass."

---

1. knock on 敲門
2. stern [stɜːrn] (a.) 堅定的
3. disapproval [ˌdɪsəˈpruːvəl] (n.) 反對
4. make one's way to 向⋯⋯走去
5. unexpectedly [ˌʌnɪkˈspektɪdli] (adv.) 意外地
6. illness [ˈɪlnəs] (n.) 疾病
7. be over 結束
8. at peace 處於和平的狀態
9. childbirth [ˈtʃaɪldbɜːrθ] (n.) 生孩子
10. mutter [ˈmʌtər] (v.) 低聲嘀咕
11. terrified [ˈterɪfaɪd] (a.) 害怕的
12. shake oneself 把自己搖醒

Vronsky went inside the house and found Anna in the hall.

"What was your husband doing here?" asked Vronsky.

"He was away, but he came back for something unexpectedly[5]," said Anna. "I'm sorry you met each other."

"Tell me about this illness[6]," said Vronsky. "Is it because you are expecting our child soon?"

Anna smiled in a gentle way. "Soon, our problems will be over[7]. We shall all be at peace[8]."

"What do you mean?" asked Vronsky.

"I will die in childbirth[9]," said Anna. "I know it. Last night, I dreamed that there was a dirty old peasant who was bending over. He was muttering[10] in French. I was so frightened. That's when I knew I would die in childbirth."

Vronsky remembered his own dream, and for a second, he was also terrified[11]. Then he shook himself[12] and said, "What nonsense! You should not believe your dreams."

The next morning, Karenin walked into Anna's bedroom without knocking.

"The only thing I asked you to do," Karenin said to Anna, "is not to receive your lover in our house. Now that you have disobeyed[1] me, I will divorce[2] you and take your son away. He will go and live at my sister's."

Anna grabbed[3] her husband's arm and cried. "Please, leave me Seriozha!"

Karenin only pulled his hand free and left the room. He went to Moscow on business[4] for three days.

In Moscow, Karenin was walking out of the office of a high government official when he heard someone calling his name. He looked around and saw Oblonsky. Karenin was not happy to see his wife's brother. Oblonsky ran over to speak with him.

"Why didn't you tell us you would be in Moscow?" he said. "We're having a dinner party

1. disobey [ˌdɪsəˈbeɪ] (v.) 違抗
2. divorce [dɪˈvɔːrs] (v.) 離婚
3. grab [ɡræb] (v.) 抓取
4. on business 為了公事
5. hesitate [ˈhezɪteɪt] (v.) 躊躇；猶豫
6. mean to 打算
7. rude [ruːd] (a.) 野蠻的
8. rumor [ˈruːmər] (n.) 謠言；傳聞
9. splendid [ˈsplendɪd] (a.) 非常好的
10. misunderstanding [ˌmɪsʌndərˈstændɪŋ] (n.) 誤會

tomorrow night. Come over between 5 and 6 o'clock."

Karenin hesitated[5]. Then he said, "I can't come to your house. I don't mean to[6] be rude[7] . . . it's just . . . I am going to divorce your sister."

Oblonsky had heard rumors[8] that there were problems between his sister and her husband. Now he knew those rumors were true, but he did not want to believe them. He said, "No, it's not possible. Anna is such a fine and splendid[9] woman. There must be some misunderstanding."

"I wish it were just a misunderstanding[10]!" replied Karenin.

**One Point**

**I wish it were** just a misunderstanding! 但願那只是誤會！

**I wish + 過去式**：wish表達一種願望，若願望與現在事實相反，動詞要用過去式。

*ex.* **I wish I had** a lot of money. 但願我有很多錢。

# Anna: An Accidental Heroine

**B**ecause *Anna Karenina* is sometimes considered as the greatest novel ever written, it is ironic[1] to consider that Tolstoy wrote it almost accidentally. At the time he started writing *Anna Karenina*, Tolstoy was actually working on another book about Peter the Great. However, he was having writer's block[2]. In this state of despair, Tolstoy remembered a story about a friend of his named Bibikov.

Bibikov lived with a woman named Anna Stepanova Pirogova. From her, Tolstoy would borrow his heroine's name and tragic death. Bibikov left Anna and decided to marry the German governess[3] who cared for his children. When Anna Stepanova heard this news, she ran away.

---

1. ironic [aɪˈrɑːnɪk] (a.) 挖苦的
2. block [blɑːk] (n.) 阻礙
3. governess [ˈɡʌvərnəs] (n.) 家庭女教師
4. wander [ˈwɑːndər] (v.) 徘徊

5. corpse [kɔːrps] (n.) 屍體
6. freight [freɪt] (n.) 貨物
7. release [rɪˈliːs] (v.) 釋放

Carrying just a bundle of clothes, she wandered[4] the countryside for three days. Then she wrote a letter to Bibikov  that read: "You are my murderer. Be happy, if an assassin can be happy. If you like, you can see my corpse[5] on the rails at Yasenki." Then she threw herself under a frieght[6] train at the Yasenki station.

Tolstoy actually went to the station the next day to witness the autopsy performed under police supervision. Looking at the doctor work over Anna's dead body, he tried to imagine the life of this poor woman. He considered the many themes of sex, duty, marriage, and moral behavior that were reflected in Russian high society at the time. From these thoughts, he began to write like water released[7] from a dam.

# CHAPTER FOUR

# Forgiveness¹

**K**arenin returned to his lonely hotel room. There he found a telegram waiting for him from Anna.

The telegram read:

> *I am dying. I beg you to come. I shall die easier with your forgiveness.*

"Is this some kind of a trick²?" asked Karenin. "But if she really is dying and I refuse to³ see her, it would be very cruel. I must return home."

Karenin knew that Anna was going to give birth to⁴ Vronsky's child soon. He guessed that Anna's health was poor because of the coming childbirth.

---

1. forgiveness [fərˈɡɪvnəs] (n.) 寬恕
2. trick [trɪk] (n.) 詭計；把戲
3. refuse to 拒絕
4. give birth to 生孩子
5. hang [hæŋ] (v.) 懸掛
6. hallway [ˈhɔːlweɪ] (n.) 走廊

When he arrived home, a servant opened the door for him.

"How is my wife?" asked Karenin.

"She gave birth to a daughter yesterday," replied the servant. "But she is very sick today. The doctors are worried."

Karenin noticed a strange hat and coat hanging[5] in the hallway[6]. "Who is here now?" he asked.

The servant hesitated for just a second. "Count Vronsky, sir."

 Check Up

What did Karenin first think when he received Anna's telegram?

ⓐ He felt pity for Anna.

ⓑ He was sure Anna was really healthy.

ⓒ He thought Anna was trying to trick him.

Ans: c

Karenin went upstairs and found Vronsky sitting outside his wife's bedroom. Vronsky had his face buried[1] in his hands. He looked up at the sound of Karenin's approach.

"She is dying," he said. "The doctors say there is no hope. Let me stay here."

Karenin turned away[2] without speaking. He went into Anna's room. She lay on her side[3], facing the door with shining eyes.

"Come here, Alexi," she said. "I do not have much time. The fever will come back, and I will die soon."

Karenin knelt down[4] beside Anna's bed. He took her warm hand in his own and put his other hand on her forehead[5]. He could feel the fever burning like a furnace[6] under her pale, white skin.

1. bury ['beri] (v.) 掩藏
2. turn away 轉過去
3. on one's side 側臥
4. kneel down 跪下
5. forehead ['fɔːrhed] (n.) 額頭
6. furnace ['fɜːrnɪs] (n.) 熔爐
7. compassion [kəm'pæʃən] (n.) 憐憫
8. chest [tʃest] (n.) 胸膛

"Stay a little, Alexi," said Anna. "There is something I must tell you. There is another woman inside of me. I am afraid of her. She is the one who fell in love with that man. I'm not that woman. I am my true self now. I'm dying. I know I am. There is only one thing that I want – forgive me. Please forgive me completely."

A warm feeling of love, compassion[7], and forgiveness filled Karenin. He laid his head on Anna's chest[8], which burned like fire through her shirt, and he cried.

---

**One Point**

She lay on her side, **facing** the door with shining eyes.
她側躺著，用閃閃發亮的眼神正對著門。

- - - - - - - - - - - - - - - - - - - - - - - - - - - - - - - - - - - - - - - - - - -

分詞構句：S + V, Ving。用分詞或是分詞片語來修飾主要句子，表示時間、
　　　　原因、條件或狀態等。
*ex.* I sat in the chair, **knitting** gloves. 我坐在椅子上織手套。

Anna saw Vronsky standing at the door.

"Why doesn't he come in?" she said. "Come in! Come in! Alexi, give him your hand."

Vronsky came in and stood by Anna's bed.

"Give him your hand," said Anna to her husband. "Forgive him."

Karenin held out[1] his hand, not even trying to stop the tears that flowed down[2] his cheeks.

"Thank God. Thank God!" cried Anna. "Now everything is done. I can die now. Oh, God, when will the pain end?"

Later, the doctor came and told Karenin that almost all patients with Anna's condition[3] died. He did not expect her to live through the night. However, the next morning, Anna's condition had not changed. The doctor said there might be some hope.

Karenin went into the small room where Vronsky had sat up all night. He took a chair opposite[4] his rival.

"I had decided on a divorce because I wanted to punish her and you,"said Karenin. "When I got her telegram, I came home with many feelings. I admit[5] I even wanted her to die. But... I saw her, and I forgave her. My duty is clear: I should stay with[6] her, and I will. If she wants to see you, I will let you know. However, I think it is best that you leave now."

---

1. hold out 維持
2. flow down 流下
3. condition [kən'dɪʃən] (n.) 情況
4. opposite ['ɑːpəzɪt] (prep.) 對面
5. admit [əd'mɪt] (v.) 承認
6. stay with 和……在一起

Vronsky could not understand how Karenin could be so calm[1] and forgiving[2]. Now he seemed like a noble gentleman: kind, honorable[3], and a better man than Vronsky. As he made his way from Karenin's house to his own home, Vronsky felt a deep sense of[4] shame, humiliation[5], and guilt[6].

He tried to sleep, but he could not. He had recently[7] been offered an important position[8] in Tashkent, but this was nothing to him now. Anna was gone, and he had been shamed by her husband.

"Am I going mad[9]?" he thought to himself. "This is how people commit suicide[10]."

Vronsky went to his desk and took out[11] a pistol. Then he pointed it at his chest and fired. As he sank[12] to the floor, he felt no pain. He saw the blood on the carpet and realized he had shot[13] himself.

---

1. calm [kɑːm] (a.) 平靜的
2. forgiving [fərˈɡɪvɪŋ] (a.) 寬容的
3. honorable [ˈɑːnərəbəl] (a.) 可敬的
4. a sense of 一種⋯⋯的感覺
5. humiliation [hjuːˌmɪliˈeɪʃən] (n.) 丟臉
6. guilt [ɡɪlt] (n.) 有罪
7. recently [ˈriːsəntli] (adv.) 最近
8. position [pəˈzɪʃən] (n.) 職位
9. go mad 失去理智
10. commit suicide 自殺
11. take out 取出

"Fool!" he thought. "I missed!"

Then everything went black[14]. His servant, who had heard the shot[15], ran in the room. Seeing the situation, he ran for the doctor. Vronsky was laid on the bed with a serious wound[16] to his chest, but his heart still beat strongly.

12. sink [sɪŋk] (v.) 倒下
13. shoot [ˈʃuːt] (v.) 發射；射中
    (shoot-shot-shot)
14. go black 變得一片黑暗
15. shot [ʃɑːt] (n.) 槍聲
16. wound [wauːnd] (n.) 傷口

Karenin had completely forgiven Anna. He pitied Vronsky, especially after he heard that Vronsky had tried to kill himself. He also pitied his son Seriozha, in whom he had not shown much interest. As time went by[1], Anna became better. Karenin noticed that she was afraid of him and would avoid[2] him if possible.

Since becoming well, Anna had forgotten what she had said to Karenin. She wanted to see Vronsky, who was recovering[3]. However, she felt a deep shame whenever she thought of her husband. Finally, she sent for[4] her brother Oblonsky.

When Oblonsky met Anna, he said, "I know it's hard, but you must cheer up. Nothing is so terrible to make you unhappy all the time."

"No, Stiva," said Anna. "I am lost[5]. But my misery[6] is not over yet . . . and the end will be terrible."

"You had the bad luck of falling in love with a man who was not your husband. Your husband forgave you, but can you continue living with him? Do you want to? Does he want to?"

"I don't know," said Anna. "I have no idea what he wants."

"Then let me sort this out[7] for you," said Oblonsky. "He's miserable; you're miserable. What good can come out of this situation? A divorce would solve everything. I will go to him now and arrange for[8] a divorce."

**Check Up**

**Fill in the blanks.**
Stiva offered to _____ _____ the miserable situation between Anna and her husband.

Ans: sort out

1. go by 過去
2. avoid [ə'vɔɪd] (v.) 避開
3. recover [rɪ'kʌvər] (v.) 恢復
4. send for 派人去叫
5. be lost 迷失
6. misery ['mɪzəri] (n.) 痛苦；不幸
7. sort out 解決
8. arrange for 安排

Oblonsky found Karenin sitting at his desk in his study.

"I hope I'm not disturbing[1] you," said Oblonsky as he entered the room. "I wanted to talk with you about my sister."

"I can think of nothing else," sighed Karenin. "Look, I have just written her this note."

Karenin handed[2] Oblonsky a short note that read:

*I can see that you are not comfortable being around me. I promised[3] you that I would forgive you with all my heart when I saw you at the time of your illness. My only desire[4] was that you would become a good wife again. But now I see that is impossible. Tell me what will make you happy and give you peace; whatever you ask, I will grant[5].*

1. disturb [dɪ'stɜːrb] (v.) 打擾
2. hand [hænd] (v.) 遞交
3. promise ['prɑːmɪs] (v.) 承諾
4. desire [dɪ'zaɪr] (n.) 渴望
5. grant [grænt] (v.) 同意
6. wonder ['wʌndər] (n.) 驚訝

Oblonsky read the note with wonder⁶. He was amazed⁷ at how generous Karenin was.

"I have to know what she wants," said Karenin.

"Well, that is simple," replied Oblonsky. "She wants a divorce. And this way, you both can have your freedom⁸."

"All right!" exclaimed Karenin. "If she desires it, I will give her a divorce, even if she takes away my son."

Oblonsky smiled gently. "Believe me, she will appreciate⁹ your generosity¹⁰. I am only doing my best to help you and her."

---

7. be amazed 吃驚
8. freedom ['friːdəm] (n.) 自由
9. appreciate [ə'priːʃieɪt] (v.) 感激

10. generosity [ˌdʒenə'rɑːsəti] (n.) 寬宏大量

Comprehension Quiz

## A True or False.

❶ Karenin decided to challenge Vronsky to a duel. ⬛T ⬛F

❷ Anna became pregnant with Vronsky's child. ⬛T ⬛F

❸ Anna gave birth to a son. ⬛T ⬛F

❹ Anna asked Karenin to forgive Vronsky, and he did. ⬛T ⬛F

❺ Vronsky tried to kill himself with a pistol. ⬛T ⬛F

❻ Karenin refused to give Anna a divorce. ⬛T ⬛F

## B Match.

❶ Anna tried to read a novel,  •

❷ Karenin took hold of his wife's arm  •

❸ Anna felt a deep shame  •

❹ Vronsky was tired,  •

❺ Vronsky felt a disagreeable sensation  •

• ⓐ so he lay down for a nap.

• ⓑ but she could not concentrate.

• ⓒ at the sight of Karenin.

• ⓓ as if she were a piece of property.

• ⓔ whenever she thought of her husband.

## Choose the correct answer.

**❶ Why did Anna finally tell Karenin that she loved Vronsky?**

    (a) Because she wanted to leave Russia with Vronsky.

    (b) Because she was pregnant with Vronsky's child.

    (c) Because Karenin told her that he still loved her.

**❷ Why did Oblonsky go to St. Petersburg to see Karenin?**

    (a) He wanted Karenin to promise to care for Anna.

    (b) He wanted to tell Karenin how to get rid of Vronsky.

    (c) He wanted to ask Karenin to give Anna a divorce.

**❸ What could Vronsky not understand about Karenin?**

    (a) How Karenin could be so calm and forgiving.

    (b) Why Karenin wanted to fight him.

    (c) Why Karenin wanted to send his son away.

## Rearrange the sentences in chronological order.

❶ Anna asks Karenin to forgive her and Vronsky.

❷ Stiva asks Karenin to divorce Anna.

❸ Anna gives birth to Vronsky's baby.

❹ Karenin returns from Moscow to St. Petersburg.

❺ Vronsky tries to commit suicide.

_____ ⇨ _____ ⇨ _____ ⇨ _____ ⇨ _____

# CHAPTER FIVE

# Escape

**V**ronsky had lain in bed on the edge of[1] death for several days after he shot himself. Slowly, he recovered. When he was well enough to move around, he decided to give up Anna. The only problem was that he could not remove[2] the sadness[3] from his heart whenever he thought of her. So when Vronsky heard from Anna's best friend, Princess Betsy, that Karenin had agreed to a divorce, he went straight over to Anna's house. Without caring if he ran into Karenin, he went to Anna's room, opened the door, and took her into his arms[4]. He showered[5] her face, neck, and shoulders with kisses.

1. on the edge of 邊緣
2. remove [rɪˈmuːv] (v.) 去掉
3. sadness [ˈsædnəs] (n.) 傷痛
4. take A into one's arms
   把 A 抱在懷裡
5. shower [ˈʃaʊər] (v.) 大量地給
6. leave all behind 拋開一切
7. tremble [ˈtrembəl] (v.) 顫抖;搖晃
8. stream down 流下來

"We will go to Europe and leave all this behind[6] us," he told Anna.

Anna trembled[7] with excitement and fear.

"Can we really live as husband and wife?" she said. "Stiva told me that my husband had agreed to a divorce. Will he really give up Seriozha?"

"Do not worry about that now. Do not think of it," replied Vronsky.

"Oh, I wish I had died," said Anna, as tears streamed down[8] her beautiful face. "It would have been easier. But I am so happy to see you again."

**One Point**

Oh, **I wish I had died**. 但願我當時就死了。

**I wish + 過去完成式**：wish 表達一種願望，若表達的願望與過去事實相反，動詞要用過去完成式。

*ex.* **I wish I had studied** hard. 但願我當時能用功一點。

Vronsky never dreamed that he would resign from[1] the military so quickly. That day, he did so without hesitation[2]. In a week, he arranged for Anna and their daughter to leave St. Petersburg. They left for Italy, thinking that Karenin would arrange for the divorce in their absence[3].

For three months, Vronsky and Anna traveled through Europe. Finally, they bought a modest[4] house in a small Italian town and lived there for three months. Anna was the happiest she

1. resign from 辭職
2. without hesitation 毫不猶豫地
3. in one's absence 在某人不在時
4. modest ['mɑːdɪst] (a.) 不大的
5. to oneself 獨佔
6. at last 最後

7. presence ['prezəns] (n.) 存在
8. constant ['kɑːnstənt] (a.) 不變的
9. source [sɔːrs] (n.) 來源
10. rarely ['rerli] (adv.) 不常
11. joyous ['dʒɔɪəs] (a.) 快樂的；高興的
12. restless ['restləs] (a.) 不耐煩的

had ever been in her life. Her health recovered completely, and the more she learned about Vronsky, the more she loved him. She had him all to herself[5] at last[6], and his presence[7] was a constant[8] source[9] of joy to her. Anna did not allow thoughts of her suffering husband or abandoned son to ruin her happiness. She had grown very fond of her daughter Ani. During these three months, she rarely[10] thought about Seriozha.

Vronsky also felt a joyous[11] sense of freedom in having left the army and his social circles. He was happy at first, but as the weeks passed, he became restless[12]. He had no job and no official duties to fill the day with. So they decided to move to Vronsky's large family estate in the countryside near St. Petersburg. But first, they planned to stop in that city so that Anna could visit her son.

### Check Up

Why did Vronsky become restless in Italy?

ⓐ He missed his family.
ⓑ He didn't have anything to do.
ⓒ He started to doubt his love for Anna.

Ans: b

When Anna left him, Karenin became very unhappy. He could not understand how he could be alone and sad after forgiving his wife and her lover. In addition[1], he felt humiliated[2] when he went out. He was sure that people were talking about him and laughing.

A few days after Anna left, he received a bill[3] from a hat store that Anna had forgotten to pay. When he saw it, an overpowering[4] sense of loss came over him. He sat down and started to cry.

There was one person in St. Petersburg who cared for[5] Karenin. She was Countess Lydia Ivanova. She was a deeply religious[6] woman who married quite young. However, her husband had left her after only two months. When she heard that Anna had gone, she pitied Karenin deeply. Now that Anna was gone, she decided to visit Karenin on the same day that he wept[7]

---

1. in addition 此外
2. humiliated [hjuːˈmɪlieɪtɪd] (a.) 丟臉的
3. bill [bɪl] (n.) 帳單
4. overpowering [ˌoʊvərˈpaʊrɪŋ] (a.) 強烈的
5. care for 喜歡
6. religious [rɪˈlɪdʒəs] (a.) 虔誠的
7. weep [wiːp] (v.) 哭泣；哀悼 (weep-wept-wept)
8. sorrow [ˈsɑːroʊ] (n.) 悲傷；傷心事

alone in his study. That was where she found Karenin, sitting with his head in both hands.

"I have heard everything!" said Lydia, as she took one of Karenin's hands into hers. "My dear friend! Your sorrow[8] is great, but you must be strong!"

✓ Check Up

Which phrase best describes Karenin's mood when he goes out in public?

a Freedom and elation

b Shame and disgrace

c Confidence and strength

Ans: b

Karenin looked up at Lydia with tears in his eyes. "It's not the loss that troubles me most," said Karenin. "I feel humiliated. Also, I find myself spending all day dealing with household matters — making arrangements[1] for the servants and my son and paying the bills."

"I understand, my dear friend," said Lydia. "You need a woman's hand in your household. Will you trust me to manage[2] your domestic[3] affairs?"

Silently, and gratefully, Karenin pressed[4] Lydia's hand.

"I will be your housekeeper," said Lydia. "We will take care of[5] Seriozha together. Don't thank me, but thank Him. Only in Him can we find peace, comfort, and love."

---

1. make arrangements 做安排
2. manage ['mænɪdʒ] (v.) 管理；處理
3. domestic [də'mestɪk] (a.) 家庭的
4. press [pres] (v.) 緊握
5. take care of 照顧
6. pat [pæt] (v.) 輕拍
7. saint [seɪnt] (n.) 聖徒；聖者
8. protect [prə'tekt] (v.) 保護

"I am very grateful to you," Karenin said.

Lydia smiled and patted[6] his hands. Then she went to Seriozha and took him in her arms. She told him that his father was a saint[7] and that his mother was dead.

When Lydia heard that Anna and Vronsky had returned to St. Petersburg, she was horrified. She felt that Karenin must be protected[8] from seeing that awful woman. He must not even know that she had come back.

**Check Up**

Fill in the blank.
Lydia was _____ at the news that Anna and Vronsky had returned to St. Petersburg.

Ans: horrified

---

**One Point**

Also, I **find myself** spending all day dealing with household matters.
還有，我發現自己整天都在處理家務。

- - - - - - - - - - - - - - - - - - - - - - - - - - - - - - - - - - - - - -

**find oneself**⋯：find + oneself + Ving / p.p. / adj. 發現自己處於某種狀態。
*ex.* He **found himself** in a small, dark room.
他發現自己在一個又小又黑的房間裡。

The next day, Lydia received a note from Anna. It read:

My dear Countess,

I am very unhappy at being apart from my son and would very much like to see him before I leave St. Petersburg. I am writing to you instead of[1] my husband because I do not wish to make him suffer by seeing me. Knowing your friendship with him, I am sure you will understand. Will you send Seriozha to me, or should I come to the house at a time when Karenin will be away? I am very grateful for your help.

Anna

---

1. instead of 代替
2. annoy [əˈnɔɪ] (v.) 惹惱
3. involve [ɪnˈvɑːlv] (v.) 使捲入；牽涉
4. evil [ˈiːvəl] (n.) 邪惡
5. sincere [sɪnˈsɪr] (a.) 真誠的
6. pray [preɪ] (v.) 祈禱
7. shock [ʃɑːk] (n.) 震驚
8. deny [dɪˈnaɪ] (v.) 拒絕接受
9. permission [pərˈmɪʃən] (n.) 允許；許可
10. reply [rɪˈplaɪ] (n.) 回覆

Lydia was very annoyed[2] by Anna's note. She decided to ignore Anna's desire not to involve[3] Karenin.

When Karenin arrived, Lydia showed him Anna's note. He read it carefully and then said, "I do not think I have the right to refuse her."

"My dear friend, you do not see the evil[4] in anyone!" exclaimed Lydia.

"I have forgiven her," replied Karenin. "I cannot refuse her love for her son."

"But is it really love?" asked Lydia. "Can she be sincere[5] in love? And should we allow her to play with the feelings of the boy? He thinks she is dead, and he prays[6] for her. Imagine his shock[7] if he were to see her!"

"I had not thought of that," said Karenin.

"If you will accept my advice, I suggest you deny[8] her the right to visit the boy," said Lydia. "With your permission[9], I will write a reply[10] saying so."

Karenin reluctantly[1] agreed, and the Countess wrote a note to Anna that read:

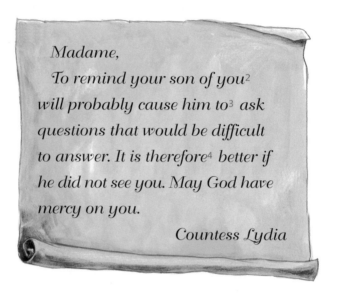

*Madame,*

*To remind your son of you[2] will probably cause him to[3] ask questions that would be difficult to answer. It is therefore[4] better if he did not see you. May God have mercy on you.*

*Countess Lydia*

Anna's response[5] to Lydia's letter was one of anger. She decided that she would go visit her son the next day, which happened to[6] be his birthday. She went in the morning, when she knew Seriozha would still be in his room. The servant who answered the door was surprised

---

1. reluctantly [rɪ'lʌktəntli] (adv.) 不情願地
2. remind A of B 使 A 想起 B
3. cause A to 導致 A
4. therefore ['ðerfɔːr] (adv.) 因此
5. response [rɪ'spɑːns] (n.) 回覆
6. happen to 發生
7. whisper ['wɪspər] (v.) 低聲說
8. split [splɪt] (v.) 使分離
9. flash [flæʃ] (v.) 閃耀
10. forward ['fɔːrwərd] (adv.) 向前

but said nothing. Anna went straight to her son's room. She found him sleeping.

"Seriozha!" she whispered[7] as she thought, "How much he has changed! He's much taller and thinner now!"

But he was the same Seriozha – her dear son. He raised himself and shook his head as if he were dreaming. He looked at his mother with confusion for a few seconds. Then his mouth split[8] into a huge smile that flashed[9] his white teeth. With joyous eyes, he fell forward[10] into his mother's arms.

✔ *Check Up*

**True or False.**

ⓐ Anna accepted Lydia's letter with resignation.  _____

ⓑ Seriozha was delighted to see his mother again. _____

Ans: a. F  b. T

"Seriozha, my darling boy!" said Anna.

"Mama!" he said. "I knew you would come on my birthday. I just knew it. I'm going to get up now. . ."

Anna was watching him, with tears flowing from her eyes.

"You didn't think I was dead, did you?" asked Anna.

"I never believed it! I knew you would come!" said Seriozha. Then he laughed. "Mama, you're sitting on my clothes!"

"Seriozha," said Anna. "You must love your father. He is kinder and better than I am. I have been wicked[1] to him. When you are older, you will understand."

"No one is better than you!" cried Seriozha.

Suddenly, the door opened, and Karenin came in. He stopped at the sight of Anna, but he showed no emotion. Seriozha sat back[2] on

---

2. wicked ['wɪkɪd] (a.) 邪惡的
2. sit back 坐好

3. bow [baʊ] (v.) 鞠躬
4. pass [pæs] (v.) 通過

the bed and began to cry. Anna kissed his wet
face and turned to go. Karenin moved back and
bowed[3] his head as she passed[4].

### Check Up

Choose the correct answer.

Anna went out of her son's room quickly because _____.

   [a] Karenin asked her to leave

   [b] she didn't want to bother Karenin

   [c] she felt her son's hatred toward her

Ans: b

### One Point

No one is better than you! 沒有人比你更好了！

主詞 + 比較級 + than：沒有什麼比……更……

*ex.* **Nothing** is **more important than** health. 沒有什麼比健康來得重要。

# Women in 19th Century Russia

I n 19th century Russia, every woman, happy or sad, was underprivileged[1] in the same ways. Even noble women such as Anna Karenina, could not have any power in government; they could not hold their own passports; they could not even attend high schools or universities. Their only goal was to marry, and marry well. Matches were made according to family background. Little attention was given to personality.

Once married, women were expected to take care of their husbands, manage the household, and give birth to children. The husbands approved or disapproved the daily business of their wives.

---

1. underprivileged [ˌʌndərˈprɪvɪlɪdʒd] (a.) 處於弱勢的
2. decency [ˈdiːsənsi] (n.) 行為準則
3. dictate [ˈdɪkteɪt] (v.) 命令
4. virgin [ˈvɜːrdʒɪn] (n.) 處女
5. obedience [əˈbiːdiəns] (n.) 服從
6. be cast out of 被趕出
7. sympathize [ˈsɪmpəθaɪz] (v.) 同情；諒解
8. hypocrisy [hɪˈpɑːkrəsi] (n.) 偽善；虛偽

A strict code of "decency[2]" applied only to women. Society dictated[3] that women be virgins[4] when they married. When  women got married, obedience[5] replaced virginity as the highest female virtue. Women who strayed outside these rules were dealt with harshly—either with violence or by being cast out of[6] society.

In Tolstoy's time, Russian intellectuals became interested in the injustice of this system. They called this "the woman question". It is interesting to note that at first, Tolstoy made Anna an ugly, evil character, but over time, changed her so that people would sympathize[7] with her and wonder at the hypocrisy[8] of a system that punished women so harshly for the same sins men committed without care.

# CHAPTER SIX

# Jealousy

Once back in her hotel room from Karenin's house, Anna cried uncontrollably[1].

"Why isn't Vronsky here in my time of need?" thought Anna. Desperately[2], she imagined that he had left her, too. "I am all alone in the world," she cried.

Quickly, she sent a message to Vronsky asking him to come at once through a hotel servant. A little while later, the servant delivered[3] a reply which said he would come back soon with a friend, Prince Yashvin.

A strange idea grew in Anna's head. "Why doesn't he come back alone? I can't tell him about my suffering if he is not alone. Does he still love me? Is he trying to avoid being alone with me? If he doesn't love me anymore, he should tell me."

However, when Vronsky and Yashvin arrived, Anna was very charming. During their conversation over dinner, Yashvin talked about politics⁴. Vronsky seemed to be very interested. Anna got the impression⁵ that Vronsky wanted to move to Moscow to run for⁶ government office.

1. uncontrollably
   [ˌʌnkənˈtroʊləbəli] (adv.) 控制不住地
2. desperately [ˈdɛspərətli]
   (adv.) 絕望地
3. deliver [dɪˈlɪvər] (v.) 傳送
4. politics [ˈpɑːlətɪks] (n.) 政治
5. impression [ɪmˈprɛʃən] (n.) 感想
6. run for 競選

After Yashvin left, Anna said, "It will be nice to live on your family's estate in the countryside."

Vronsky hesitated and seemed a little guilty.

"Actually, my mother is currently[1] staying there," he replied. "It would not be proper[2] for us to live there while she is there. Besides[3], we should wait for the divorce."

Anna felt lost. In the next few days, Vronsky would go out to dinner parties or to the opera without her. She could not go because she would be the subject[4] of much gossip. However, Vronsky needed to go there to make important connections. He had decided to become a politician[5].

---

1. currently ['kɜːrəntli] (adv.) 目前
2. proper ['prɑːpər] (a.) 適合的
3. besides [bɪ'saɪdz] (adv.) 此外
4. subject ['sʌbdʒɪkt] (n.) 主題
5. politician [ˌpɑːlə'tɪʃən] (n.) 政治家
6. princess ['prɪnses] (n.) 公主

During this time, Anna became jealous. She imagined Vronsky meeting many young and beautiful women at these social events. She was afraid he might fall in love with another woman. This was actually her worst fear because Vronsky had once told her, without thinking, that his mother wanted him to marry the young Princess[6] Sorokina.

✓ Check Up

Anna could not go to social functions because _____.

   ⓐ  she was not invited

   ⓑ  everyone would talk about her

   ⓒ  she was afraid of meeting Karenin

Ans: b

One evening, Anna became tired of staying at home by herself[1] and went to an opera. During the performance, a member of the royal[2] family, who was sitting next to her, said hello. Anna had known him for a long time. Suddenly, his wife stood up and said she would not be seen with such a wicked woman as Anna. The wife left abruptly[3], and her husband followed. All he could do was nod to Anna in pity. Most of the audience in the opera house saw this incident[4]. Anna was extremely[5] humiliated. She stayed as long as she could, frozen[6] in her seat. After a few minutes, she went back to her hotel room and cried.

---

1. by oneself 單獨地
2. royal ['rɔɪəl] (a.) 王室的；盛大的
3. abruptly [ə'brʌptli] (adv.) 突然地
4. incident ['ɪnsɪdənt] (n.) 事件
5. extremely [ɪk'striːmli] (adv.) 非常
6. frozen ['froʊzən] (v.) 結凍

✔ Check Up

## What happened at the opera house?

[a] A man told her she should be ashamed of herself.

[b] She tripped and fell on the opera house stairs.

[c] An important woman said Anna was a bad person.

Ans: c

Anna was waiting for Vronsky to return from a dinner party. They had argued the day before, and Vronsky had been away from home the entire day. Anna was feeling miserable[1] and lonely, and she decided to forgive him everything so that they could be friends again.

When Vronsky came in, she said, "Well, did you have a good time?"

Vronsky could see that Anna was in a good mood, so he said, "The same as usual."

"Darling," said Anna, "I went for a drive[2] today. It was so lovely, and it reminded me of the country. Your mother has moved to her country house by Moscow, so your estate is empty. We can wait for the divorce in the country."

"Yes, I agree," said Vronksy. "When do you think we should go?"

---

1. miserable ['mɪzərəbəl] (a.)
   痛苦的；悽慘的
2. go for a drive 出去走走

3. embarrassed [ɪm'bærəst] (a.)
   尷尬的
4. suspiciously [sə'spɪʃəsli] (adv.)
   可疑地

"How about the day after tomorrow?" suggested Anna.

"Yes. Oh, actually, no," said Vronsky. "The day after tomorrow is Sunday, and I must visit my mother."

He felt a little embarrassed[3] because Anna was looking at him suspiciously[4].

"You could go there tomorrow," Anna said.

"No. I'm going to my mother's on business — to take some money from her," replied Vronsky. "It won't be ready by tomorrow."

"Well then, we won't go to the country at all!" said Anna.

"Why not?" asked Vronsky in surprise. "We can go there in a few days!"

1. postpone [poʊstˈpoʊn] (v.)
延期；延遲
2. accuse A of 指責 A 某事

3. childbirth [ˈtʃaɪldbɜːrθ] (n.) 生孩子
4. wipe out 抹去

100

"No," said Anna. "If you loved me, you would want to go immediately. And if you don't love me anymore, it would be better and more honest to say so!"

She turned to leave, but Vronsky grabbed her hand.

"Wait," he said. "I don't understand. I said we must postpone[1] our departure for a few days, and you accuse me of[2] not loving you any more."

Without looking at him, Anna pulled her hand away from him and left the room.

"He hates me. That is clear," thought Anna. "He is in love with another woman."

Thinking back to her illness during childbirth[3], Anna thought it would have been much better if she had died then.

"If I die, then all the shame and disgrace I have brought on my husband and Seriozha will be wiped out[4]," thought Anna. "And if I die, he too will be sorry."

Check Up

**Fill in the blank.**

Vronsky told Anna that they had to _____ their departure to the country.

Ans: postpone

The next morning, as Anna and Vronsky were having breakfast, a telegram arrived for him. He read it and seemed to be hiding it from Anna. She asked who it was from.

"It's from Stiva," he said.

"Why don't you show it to me?" asked Anna.

"All right," said Vronsky reluctantly. "Read it yourself."

The telegram read:

*Have seen Karenin, but little hope of divorce.*

---

1. frustrated ['frʌstreɪtɪd] (a.) 沮喪的
2. definite ['defɪnət] (a.) 明確的；一定的
3. get upset 生氣
4. uncertain [ʌn'sɜːrtn] (a.) 猶豫的
5. in one's power 在某人的掌握之中

Anna said, "There was no need to hide this from me. A divorce doesn't interest me. Why does it interest you?"

Vronsky felt frustrated[1]. "Because I like things to be definite[2]," he said. "And I think the reason you get upset[3] so easily is because your position is uncertain[4]."

"My position is certain," replied Anna. "I am completely in your power[5]. It's your position that is not sure."

"Anna, if you think I want to be free. . ." Vronsky started to say.

Anna interrupted him, "I really do not care what your mother thinks and whom she wants you to marry."

True or False.

[a] The telegram was from Karenin. _____

[b] Vronsky doesn't care about Anna getting a divorce. _____

Ans: a. F  b. F

"We are not talking about that!" shouted[1] Vronsky.

"Yes, we are," replied Anna. "And let me tell you I do not care about the heartless[2] woman, whether she is old or not, and I do not want to have anything to do with[3] her!"

Vronsky became very cold and angry. "Anna, please do not speak about my mother like that. Show some respect."

Anna spent the whole day in her room. Again, the thought of death came into her mind[4] as the only solution to her problems. Nothing mattered to her now – whether they went to the country or not. All that mattered was to punish Vronsky. Anna laid down for a nap and had the same strange dream about the dirty peasant muttering in French.

1. shout [ʃaʊt] (v.) 喊叫
2. heartless ['hɑːrtləs] (a.) 無情的
3. have to do with 與……有關
4. come into one's mind 忽然想起
5. with a start 吃驚地
6. lean out 探出身體

She woke with a start[5] and heard a carriage outside. Looking out the window, she saw a young, pretty girl lean out[6]. Vronsky ran out of the house and took a package from the girl. He said something, and she smiled. Then her carriage drove off, and Vronsky came back inside.

Trembling with fear and anger, Anna went
to Vronsky's study. She decided to tell him she
would leave him.

"That was Princess Sorokina," said Vronsky.
"She brought me some documents[1] from my
mother. We are going to visit her tomorrow,
aren't we?"

"You are, but I am not," said Anna. She started
to leave.

"Anna, we cannot continue like this. . ."

"You will be sorry for[2] this," said Anna, and
she left.

Vronsky saw the despair in Anna's eyes. He
got up to follow her, but then he sat down again.

"No," he thought. "I've done everything I can.
She needs to be left alone[3] now."

He sent for a carriage and prepared to visit
his mother alone. The carriage arrived a few
minutes later, and he left the house.

---

1. document ['dɑːkjʊmənt] (n.)
   公文；文件
2. be sorry for 對……感到抱歉
3. be left alone 獨處
4. grip [grɪp] (v.) 緊握；夾住

Anna saw him leave through her window. A sudden horror gripped[4] her heart.

"He has left me! It's all over now!" she thought.

Quickly, she ran downstairs. "Where has he gone?" she asked a servant.

"To the railway station," came the reply. "He is going to catch a train to Obiralovka."

Check Up

What does Vronsky decide to do about Anna?

a He decides to give her some time alone.

b He decides to try to convince her that he loves her.

c He decides to talk to his mother about their situation.

Ans: a

Obiralovka was the district[1] where Vronsky's mother lived. Anna sat down and quickly wrote a note:

> It's all my fault. Come back home. We must talk. For God's sake[2], come back! I am very frightened.

The servant took the note. Half an hour later, he came back and said he was too late in getting to[3] the train station. Vronsky had already left. Quickly, she wrote out a telegram and told the servant to send it.

1. district ['dɪstrɪkt] (n.) 區
2. for God's sake 看在上帝的份上
3. get to 趕到
4. absolutely [ˌæbsəˈluːtli] (adv.) 絕對

5. meaningless ['miːnɪŋləs] (a.) 毫無意義的
6. coachman ['koʊtʃmən] (n.) 馬車夫

It read:

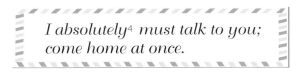

> *I absolutely⁴ must talk to you;*
> *come home at once.*

"I must go there right now to talk to him," Anna thought.

She looked at the railway time schedule and saw that a train left for Obiralovka in an hour. She sent for a carriage and went to the train station. On the way, she looked at the people on the streets. Their lives seemed meaningless⁵ to her. At the station, the coachman⁶ asked, "Should I buy a ticket to Obiralovka for you?"

"Yes," said Anna. She looked at the other people waiting for the train and did not like any of them.

---

**One Point**

Vronsky **had** already **left**. 馮斯基已經離開了。

過去完成式（**had + p.p.**）：用來表示在過去某個特定時間之前，一個已經完成的行為動作。

*ex.* I gave him the book which I **had bought**. 我給了他我之前買的書。

When she got her ticket, Anna boarded[1] the train. She thought the other people in the carriage were looking at her in a strange and unpleasant way. Anna looked out the window and saw a dirty old peasant bending down and looking at the carriage wheels[2].

"There's something familiar about that peasant," thought Anna. Then the train started. When she arrived in Obiralovka, Anna got out and asked the telegram clerk if there was a note from Count Vronsky for her.

"Yes, ma'am," replied the clerk. "I just got it. Here it is. Actually, Count Vronsky's coachman was just here to pick up Princess Sorokina."

Anna read the note that Vronsky had written carelessly[3]. It read:

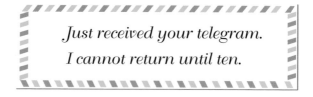

*Just received your telegram.*
*I cannot return until ten.*

1. board [bɔːrd] (v.) 上（車、船、飛機等）
2. wheel [wiːl] (n.) 輪子
3. carelessly [ˈkerləsli] (adv.) 草率地
4. wander [ˈwɑːndər] (v.) 漫遊；閒逛

"Yes, this is what I expected!" thought Anna. She thought how awkward it would be to walk into Vronsky's mother's house with Princess Sorokina there.

"Oh, where shall I go?" she thought as she wandered[4] down the platform. She wanted to be alone, and there was no one at the end of the platform. Another train was approaching, and the platform began to shake.

**Check Up**

**Fill in the blank.**

Anna thought it would be _____ to walk into Vronsky's mother's house when Princess Sorokina was there.

Ans: awkward

Suddenly, Anna remembered the man who had been run over[1] by a train on the day she met Vronsky. Now she knew what she had to do. Quickly, she walked down the steps to the tracks[2]. She looked at the wheels of the approaching train.

"There," she thought. "There in the middle between the wheels. I will kneel down there. I will punish him and escape from my pitiful[3] existence."

Anna missed the first carriage, but on the second, she dropped to her knees[4]. As soon as the wheels of this carriage passed, she knelt forward, over the rail[5]. At that same moment, she was filled with horror at the thought of[6] what she was doing.

"Where am I? What am I doing? Why?" she suddenly thought.

1. run over 輾過
2. track [træk] (n.) 軌道
3. pitiful ['pɪtɪfəl] (a.) 卑微的
4. drop to one's knees 跪下
5. rail [reɪl] (n.) 鐵軌
6. at the thought of 一想到

7. strike [straɪk] (v.) 打；擊
   (strike-struck-struck)
8. drag [dræg] (v.) 拖
   (drag-dragged-dragged)
9. push down 向下推
10. dim [dɪm] (a.) 微暗的

She tried to get up and throw herself back, but something huge struck[7] her on the back of her head. It dragged[8] her along the rail and pushed her down[9].

"God, forgive me for everything!" she thought.

A dirty peasant working on the rails on the other side of the train was talking to himself quietly. He did not see Anna as she was pushed along the opposite rail. The light inside her mind by which she had viewed all her troubles, all her lies, sorrow, and evil, suddenly became very bright. For the first time, she clearly saw everything that had been hidden from her in darkness. But just as quickly, that light grew dim[10] and was lost forever.

# Comprehension Quiz

## A Fill in the blanks with the given words.

completely    rarely    deeply    gratefully    suddenly

❶ While in Italy, Anna _____ thought about her son.

❷ Karenin _____ accepted Lydia's offer.

❸ Anna's health recovered _____ while she was in Italy.

❹ Lydia's rejection hurt Anna _____.

❺ _____, Anna remembered the man run over by a train.

## B Match.

❶ And if you don't love
me anymore,
• ⓐ and I must visit my
mother.

❷ I think the reason you
get upset so easily
• ⓑ about my mother like
that.

❸ Anna, please do not speak •
• ⓒ it would be better and more
honest to say so!

❹ The day after tomorrow
is Sunday,
• ⓓ is because your position
is uncertain.

❺ It will be nice •
• ⓔ to live on your family's estate
in the countryside.

## C  Choose the correct answer.

**1** What did Vronsky become interested in after quitting his job?

(a) Horse racing     (b) Farming     (c) Politics

**2** What did Lydia do with Anna's note?

(a) She showed it to Karenin.

(b) She threw it away.

(c) She returned it to Anna without reading it.

**3** Why did Vronsky want Karenin to give Anna a divorce?

(a) Because he liked things to be definite.

(b) Because he wanted to leave Anna.

(c) Because then Anna could bring her son to live with them.

## D  Make sentences with given words.

**1** Karenin looked up at Lydia _____.

(tears, in, with, eyes, his )

**2** Anna was _____ in her life.

(ever, happiest, she, been, the, had)

**3** The servant who _____.

(was, door, answered, the, surprised)

# Guide to Listening Comprehension

*Use your book's CD to enjoy the audio version of* ***Anna Karenina.*** *When listening to the story, use some of the techniques shown below. If you take time to study some phonetic characteristics of English, listening will be easier.*

## Get in the flow of English.

English creates a rhythm formed by combinations of strong and weak stress intonations. Each word has its particular stress that combines with other words to form the overall pattern of stress or rhythm in a particular sentence.

When speaking and listening to English, it is essential to get in the flow of the rhythm of English. It takes a lot of practice to get used to such a rhythm. So, you need to start by identifying the stressed syllable in a word.

## Listen for the strongly stressed words and phrases.

In English, key words and phrases that are essential to the meaning of a sentence are stressed louder. Therefore, pay attention to the words stressed with a higher pitch. When listening to an English recording for the first time, what matters most is to listen for a general understanding of what you hear. Do not try to hear every single word. Most of the unstressed words are articles or auxiliary verbs, which don't play an important role in the general context. At this level, you can ignore them.

## Pay attention to liaisons.

In reading English, words are written with a space between them. There isn't such an obvious guide when it comes to listening to English. In oral English, there are many cases when the sounds of words are linked with adjacent words.

For instance, let's think about the phrase "take off," which can be used in "take off your clothes." "Take off your clothes" doesn't sound like [teɪk ɔːf] with each of the words completely and clearly separated from the others. Instead, it sounds as if almost all the words in context are slurred together, [ˈteɪkɔːf], for a more natural sound.

## Shadow the voice of the native speaker.

Finally, you need to mimic the voice of the native speaker. Once you are sure you know how to pronounce all the words in a sentence, try to repeat them like an echo. Listen to the book again, but this time you should try a fun exercise while listening to the English.

This exercise is called "shadowing." The word "shadow" means a dark shade that is formed on a surface. When used as a verb, the word refers to the action of following someone or something like a shadow. In this exercise, pretend you are a parrot and try to shadow the voice of the native speaker.

Try to mimic the reader's voice by speaking at the same speed, with the same strong and weak stresses on words, and pausing or stopping at the same points.

Experts have already proven this technique to be effective. If you practice this shadowing exercise, your English speaking and listening skills will improve by leaps and bounds. While shadowing the native speaker, don't forget to pay attention to the meaning of each phrase and sentence.

**1** step — Listen to what you want to shadow many times. Start out by just trying to shadow a few words or a sentence.

**2** step — Mimic the CD out loud. You can shadow everything the speaker says as if you are singing a round, or you also can speak simultaneously with the recorded voice of the native speaker.

**3** step — As you practice more, try to shadow more. For instance, shadow a whole sentence or paragraph instead of just a few words.

# APPENDIX ❷

# Listening Guide

Happy families are all alike, but unhappy families are unhappy in their own unique ways.

The Oblonsky household was one such unhappy family. Dolly, the wife, had ( ❶ ) ( ) three days ago that her husband was having an affair with the French ( ❷ ). She announced that she ( ❸ ) ( ) go on living in the same house with her husband. She had stayed in her room, and her husband, Prince Stepan Oblonsky, had stayed away from home during the day. Their five children ran wild ( ❹ ) ( ) house. The cook quit, and the other servants were thinking of doing the same.

On the third morning after the quarrel, Prince Oblonsky, who was called Stiva by his friends, ( ❺ ) ( ) on the leather couch in his study. He had just had a wonderful dream, and he was smiling as he reached up for his robe. Suddenly, he realized that he was in his study and his robe was in his wife's bedroom. The ( ❻ ) ( ) ( ) face vanished.

以下為《安娜‧卡列尼娜》各章節前半部。一開始若能聽清楚發音，之後就沒有聽力的負擔。首先，請聽過摘錄的章節，之後再反覆聆聽括弧內單字的發音，並仔細閱讀各種發音的說明。以下都是以英語的典型發音為基礎，所做的簡易說明，即使這裡未提到的發音，也可以配合 CD 反覆聆聽，如此一來聽力必能更上層樓。

**❶ found out**：found 以 d 結尾，接上以母音為字首的 out ，便形成連音 foundout。

**❷ tutor**：tutor 中有兩個 t，而它們之間只隔了一個 u ，因此發音時後面的 t 會和 or 的發音結合。

**❸ could not**：could、would、should，這三個字的 oul 輕讀時都發 [ə]，重讀時才發 [ʊ]。一般而言，除非是要強調這幾個字，否則都是輕讀。尤其是否定句，後面接 not 時，重音會在 not，所以這三個字必定輕讀，同時因為 not 的字首是子音 n ，所以前字字尾的 d 幾乎聽不出來。

**❹ around the**：around 和 the 連在一起發音時，around 的 [d] 和 the 的 [ð] 會產生連音。

**❺ woke up**：由於 woke 的發音以 [k] 結尾，當後面接上 up 時就會形成連音，唸起來像是 wokup。

**❻ smile on his**：h 的發音往往都相當微弱，his 中 h 就不太發音或是相當微弱。

"It's all my fault," Stiva thought. "Dolly will never forgive me! What have I done? But the real ( ❶ ) is that I cannot really be blamed!"

Stiva remembered how he had come home from the theater three nights ago. He had found his wife in their upstairs bedroom with a letter from the French tutor in her hand. The memory of the ( ❷ ) ( ) ( ) on his wife's face and the tears in her eyes still stabbed his heart.

The affair with the French tutor was not the ( ❸ ) ( ) Stiva. He was ( ❹ ) years old and was quite handsome and charming. Women younger than his wife were constantly attracted to him. The biggest problem was that he was no longer in love with his wife. She was a good wife and mother, but she was no longer a beautiful young woman.

Stiva rang the bell for his servant, who came in with a telegram. Stiva opened it, and his face quickly brightened when he read the contents. His sister, Anna, was coming for a visit. Anna lived in ( ❺ ) with her husband and eight-year-old son. Dolly really liked Anna. Stiva had invited his sister to visit and try to solve the current situation. The telegram said that Anna ( ❻ ) ( ) ( ) Moscow by train later today.

1. **tragedy**：tragedy 的音標為 [ˈtrædʒədi]，不過其實 tr 的發音聽起來很像是 [tʃ]，tree 的發音也是同樣的道理。

2. **look of pain**：of 變化成 a 的音，因此 look of 聽起來就像 looka。

3. **first for**：這兩個字接在一起時，為了清楚讀出 for 字首的子音，若前一個字的字尾也為子音，通常會含糊帶過，first 接 f，聽起來很像 firsfor。

4. **thirty-four**：含有 ty 的數字，重音要在第一個音節上；有 teen 的數字則是重音落在 teen 上。

5. **St. Petersburg**：這兩個字接在一起時，為了清楚讀出 Petersburg 字首的子音，若前一個字的字尾也為子音，通常會含糊帶過，St. 接 p，聽起來很像 Sain Petersburg。

6. **would arrive in**：字尾以 d 音結束的單字，如果後面接一個以 a 起頭的單字，唸起來就不會完全是 da 的音，而是一種介於 da 和 ta 之間的音。而 arrive 以 v 音結束，後接以母音為首的 in，也會形成連音唸起來像 arrivin。

# istening Comprehension

### A Listen to the CD and write down the numbers.

ⓐ Anna          ⓑ Karenin          ⓒ Stiva          ⓓ Vronsky

_____          _____          _____          _____

### B Listen to the CD and fill in the blanks.

❶ Stiva _____ many _____ with pretty young women.

❷ Anna _____ Dolly not to _____ Stiva.

❸ Karenin could feel the _____ burning like a _____ under Anna's skin.

❹ Vronsky told Anna they must _____ an _____ to their secrecy.

❺ Anna _____ that she _____ loved her husband.

❻ At the _____, Kitty could see that Vronsky and Anna were _____ to each other.

❼ For the _____ _____, Anna saw everything clearly.

## C Listen to the CD and choose the correct answer.

**❶** _____?

   (a) Giving birth to a baby girl
   (b) Traveling to Italy
   (c) A dirty old peasant

**❷** _____?

   (a) Because he felt that Karenin had shamed him.
   (b) Because Anna was going to give birth to his baby.
   (c) Because he thought his career was ruined.

## D Listen to the CD. True or False.

**❶** _____   T  F
**❷** _____   T  F
**❸** _____   T  F
**❹** _____   T  F

# Answers

p.42    A ❶ (b) ❷ (a) ❸ (d) ❹ (c)

        B ❶ decide if ❷ think of ❸ got along ❹ stay away ❺ relied on

p.43    C ❶ (b) ❷ (c) ❸ (a)        D ❺→❶→❸→❷→❹

p.74    A ❶ F ❷ T ❸ F ❹ T ❺ T ❻ F    B ❶ (b) ❷ (d) ❸ (e) ❹ (a) ❺ (c)

p.75    C ❶ (b) ❷ (c) ❸ (a)        D ❸→❹→❶→❺→❷

p.114   A ❶ rarely ❷ gratefully ❸ completely ❹ deeply ❺ Suddenly

        B ❶ (c) ❷ (d) ❸ (b) ❹ (a) ❺ (e)

p.115   C ❶ (c) ❷ (a) ❸ (a)

        D ❶ with tears in his eyes ❷ the happiest she had ever been
          ❸ answered the door was surprised

p.124   A ❶ A lazy but charming man who likes to enjoy life - (c)
          ❷ A capable military man who gives up his career for love - (d)
          ❸ A woman who leaves a cold husband, but cannot find lasting
            happiness - (a)
          ❹ A strict man who has trouble showing his emotions - (b)

        B ❶ bad, affairs ❷ advised, leave ❸ fever, furnace ❹ put, end
          ❺ realized, never ❻ ball, attracted ❼ first, time

p.125   C ❶ What did Anna dream about before she committed suicide?
            (c)
          ❷ What did Vronsky try to kill himself? (a)

        D ❶ At first, Vronsky's mother really liked Anna. (T)
          ❷ It was not easy for Anna to leave her husband because she
            loved her son. (T)
          ❸ In this story, Anna is the only person who was killed by a
            train. (F)
          ❹ Lydia helped Karenin because she wanted to be his wife. (F)

126

# 安娜‧卡列尼娜 —————————— 中譯文

Leo Tolstoy (1828-1910)

## 人物介紹

p.8-9

**安娜**：我是一位來自俄國上流社會的有錢婦女。雖然我已經生過一個兒子了，但我的青春美貌猶在。我的丈夫姓卡列寧，是一位重要的政府官員。他有時很冷漠，情感缺乏熱情。在我去莫斯科探訪我的哥哥時，我才發現自己原來是不快樂的。在莫斯科，我遇到了一個男人，他改變了我的一生……。

**馮斯基**：我是一名俄國軍官。我家境富裕，前途無量。但獨獨有一件事卻可能讓我身敗名裂，那就是，我不可自拔地愛上了一名美麗的女子。不過即使如此，我仍不失為是一位高尚的人。「榮譽」對我來說非常重要。

**卡列寧**：我是一位公務繁重的政府官員。我的工作和身分對我來說，至為重要。我已婚，娶了一位美貌的女子。我深愛著她，也認為她過得很幸福，會與我終生廝守。

**史帝沃**：我在政府單位裡上班，但這只是份工作，不是我的生命。人生苦短，不要把光陰蹉跎在你不喜歡的事情上。我總是能撥出時間來和朋友今朝有酒今朝醉。那把馬子呢？當然囉，我韻事不斷，儘管我已經結婚啦。

**朵麗**：啊，我的丈夫，我深愛的史帝沃，竟然和我們的法國保姆有染！我好慘啊！我該怎麼辦？啊，史帝沃已經邀請他的妹妹安娜來和我談，這樣也好，安娜對這種事很有想法。

## 第一章　不幸福的家庭

p.10-11 幸福的家庭，大同小異；不幸福的家庭，則各有各的不幸之處。

歐隆斯基這一家，就是這樣一個不幸福的家庭。三天前，女主人朵麗發現了自己的老公和法國來的家庭教師有染，於是她說自己再也無法和丈夫再待在同一個屋簷下了。她把自己關在房間裡，而她的老公「史帝龐・歐隆斯基親王」，則在東窗事發當天之後就沒回家了。他們的五名兒女，在屋子裡東奔西跑，玩瘋了。廚師已經辭職，其他的僕人也想跟進。

在爭吵後的第三天早上，被朋友暱稱為「史帝沃」的歐隆斯基親王，在書房的皮沙發上醒來。他剛做了個美夢，當他伸手要拿睡袍時，還一邊笑著。這時，他突然意識到自己躺在書房裡，而他的睡袍是放在妻子的臥室裡。他臉上的笑容頓時消失。

p.12-13「都怪我，朵麗不可能會原諒我的！」史帝沃心想：「我幹了什麼蠢事啊？真正的悲劇是，又不能都歸咎於我啊。」

史帝沃想起了三天之前的那個晚上，他是如何從劇院回到家中的。當時他在樓上的臥室裡，看到妻子的手上拿著一封法國女家教所寫的信。他記得妻子臉上的痛苦神情，還有她眼裡的淚水，這些仍刺痛著他的心。

和法國女教師有染，並不是史帝沃第一次的出軌。他今年 34 歲，長得很帥，很有魅力。他總是吸引了比妻子年輕的女子。最大的問題是，他對妻子的愛情已逝。妻子是一個賢妻良母，但她的青春與美貌不再。

史帝沃按鈴叫了僕人，僕人拿了一封電報走進來。史帝沃打開電報，他看了看，神情很快地愉悅了起來。他的妹妹安娜，就要來看他了。安娜住在聖彼得堡，有一個八歲大的兒子。朵麗很喜歡安娜，所以史帝沃就找妹妹來幫他應付他現在的難題。電報上說，今天稍晚，安娜就會搭火車抵達莫斯科了。

p.14-15史帝沃換了衣服，走出書房的門，來到了妻子的臥室裡。妻子當時正在思索著是否要打包行李，帶著孩子離開。她很憤怒，但史帝沃畢竟是她的丈夫，她心裡頭還是愛著這個老公的。

「安娜今天會到達。」史帝沃輕聲說道。

「噢，那又怎樣？我不見她！」朵麗叫道：「我要帶著孩子離開這個家，那樣你就可以讓你的情婦住進來了！」

「朵麗，請妳明白……」史帝沃說。

「明白？你這個可惡、可恨的人！」

「朵麗，請想想孩子們吧！沒有父親陪伴他們長大，他們就完了。你不要懲罰他們，你要懲罰的是我！做錯事情的人是我。」史帝沃懇求道。

朵麗站著不發一語，逕自走向房門。

「朵麗，讓我再說一句話……」史帝沃說這話時，朵麗打開了房門。

「滾出去！」朵麗叫道，接著把門甩上轉過身去。

史帝沃悽悽然地走下樓，在吩咐僕人幫安娜準備房間後，便出門前往位於莫斯科的官府大樓上班。

p.16-17 史帝沃以前是個聰明的學生，只是很懶惰，而且很皮。後來，他靠著父親在俄國權貴中的名氣和人脈，在官府裡謀得一份高薪的職位。史帝沃不是那種野心勃勃的男人，在工作上也不認真。他靠的是自己迷人的風采和機智來擄獲人心。

中午時，在史帝沃正走出會議時，他看到一名寬肩的男人踩著輕快的腳步跑上樓，朝著他過來。

「雷文，真意外見到你啊！你怎麼來莫斯科啦？」史帝沃問。

「我有事情要問你。」雷文說完，突然露出一副害羞的樣子，「你知道席巴斯基家最近在做什麼嗎？」

史帝沃立刻明白了雷文回來莫斯科的原因。他早就知道，雷文和朵麗的小妹凱蒂・席巴斯基郡主，他們兩個人在談戀愛。

「席巴斯基家今晚八點要辦一場晚宴，我會派一名僕人過去跟他們說你人已經在莫斯科了。」史帝沃笑著說：「當然啦，你會被邀請去參加，凱蒂也會在。現在，我們先去打點午餐吧。」

p.18-19 在用午餐時，史帝沃問道：「你怎麼離開莫斯科這麼久？又為什麼突然跑回來？」

「跟你猜的一樣，我和凱蒂在談戀愛。我會離開莫斯科，是因為我想凱蒂是不會答應嫁給我的。她媽媽看來並不喜歡我。不過，我就是很想凱蒂。」雷文嘆著氣說，接著突然激動地說：「我是回來跟凱蒂求婚的，你想她有可能答應我的求婚嗎？」

史帝沃回答：「當然有可能啊，朵麗跟我說，她覺得凱蒂是愛你的。」

「那太好了！」雷文叫道，一副鬆了口氣且喜出望外的樣子。

「只是你一定要知道一件事，」史帝沃說：「你有一個情敵！那個人就是馮斯基伯爵，他是一個年輕的騎兵軍官，背景很強。凱蒂的媽媽也中意他，不過我想凱蒂比較喜歡你。今天晚宴上，你要比馮斯基早到，然後跟凱蒂求婚。祝你好運啦！」

史帝沃離開前往車站接安娜，雷文則回到自己的公寓裡。

Saint Petersburg

在安娜·卡列尼娜生活的時代裡，聖彼得堡是俄國的首都。在19世紀，聖彼得堡是全俄國最重要且最美麗的城市。這座城市於1704年由「彼得大帝」所興建，以當作通往歐洲的門戶。

這座城市臨芬蘭灣，是前往北歐國家的水路要道。彼得大帝和同盟者為自己興建了大皇宮，皇宮至今仍然矗立著。城裡到處可見裝飾華麗的莊嚴教堂聳立在房舍和官府大廈之中。

阿姆斯特丹市和威尼斯市給了彼得大帝靈感，讓他決定在涅瓦河岸建造花崗石河堤；如今，在城裡，這條河有許多運河蜿蜒著。在彼得大帝的想像中，人民到處都可以搭到船，所以他禁止建造永久性的橋。一直到了1850年，才首度開始造橋。

這座城市成了「俄羅斯之珠」，而托爾斯泰故事中的女主角安娜，則是聖彼得堡之珠。把安娜這個角色的生活設定在聖彼得堡，是很恰到好處的安排，因為她的丈夫是一名有野心的高級官員，當然會來俄國的首都求發展。還有，聖彼得堡也是俄國社會發展最精緻的代表——那裡有各種歌劇院、舞廳和俄國的上流社會。

俄國沒有其他的城市，會比聖彼得堡更適合當作《安娜·卡列尼娜》的場景設定背景。

## 第二章 意外的邂逅

`p.22-23` 歐隆斯基在車站等待從聖彼得堡開來的火車時，巧遇了馮斯基伯爵。

「你在等誰啊？」馮斯基問。

「我是來接一位美麗的女子的，」史帝沃答道：「我妹，安娜啦。」

「喔，是卡列寧的夫人嗎？」馮斯基問。

「是啊，你認識她？」

「不，我不認識，我沒有印象。」馮斯基說。

「卡列寧」這個姓氏，讓馮斯基聯想到是正經八百的無趣之輩。

「那你一定知道我那位備受尊敬的妹婿吧，他是一位高官。」史帝沃說道。

「我知道，他名聲響亮，而且很有雄心。我知道他這個人很聰明，而且對信仰很虔誠。總之我呢，是來接我母親的。」

這時火車進站的聲音，中斷了他們的談話。在火車就要停止時，馮斯基的旁邊跳下一位年輕的列車員。馮斯基詢問馮斯基伯爵夫人的車廂，列車員指了指，馮斯基於是朝車廂門走過去。當他走到車門前，他挪身站在一旁，讓一位女士下車。

p.24-25 馮斯基看了女士一眼，看出她是一位有錢的夫人。他往她靠近了些，在她美麗的臉龐上瞧了瞧，覺得她的長相好像有什麼特別的。就在他盯著她瞧時，她也看了看他，露出友善中帶點不解的神情。

馮斯基對她點了點頭後就走進車廂。他的母親，一位黑眼捲髮的老婦人，她一口薄唇，對他露出微笑。

「你收到我的電報了囉。」她問：「你身體還好吧？」

「你這一路還好嗎？」馮斯基坐到母親的身邊，問道。就在這時候，馮斯基女士看到剛下車的人走回了車廂，一臉困惑的樣子。

「妳找到妳哥哥了嗎？」馮斯基伯爵夫人問。

馮斯基頓時明白了這一位就是歐隆斯基的妹妹，安娜‧卡列尼娜。

「您哥哥剛剛就在外面那裡，」馮斯基說：「您在這裡等一下，我去找他過來。」

安娜笑了笑，然後在伯爵夫人的身邊坐下。馮斯基走出車廂，在人群中找到了歐隆斯基。他喊他過來，說道：「你妹妹在這個車廂裡，和我母親坐在一塊兒。」

p.26-27 安娜從車窗看到了哥哥，便立即下車廂，她跑向哥哥抱住他，熱情地親吻他的雙頰。馮斯基則扶著母親走下車廂。

「她很迷人，是吧？」伯爵夫人對兒子說道。接著，她對安娜說：「我都這把年紀了，說話也沒什麼好忌諱的了。我要跟妳說啊，我被妳迷住啦。」

安娜聽了很開心。她親吻了伯爵夫人，然後把手伸出去給馮斯基。馮斯基親吻了她的手，心情感到非常愉快。

就在這時，突然一陣騷動，站長和幾位列車員從一旁跑了過去。他們的臉色蒼白，一副受到驚嚇的樣子。馮斯基建議兩位女士先回到車廂，然後他和史帝沃就跟著車站的人員跑到了火車頭。

有一位警衛在車站進站時被輾死於車輪下了。史帝沃一看到屍體，就顯得很難過，眼淚都快要掉下來了。

「喔，太可怕了！」他喊道。

馮斯基和史帝沃幫不上什麼忙，兩人就走回車廂，安娜和伯爵夫人正在那裡等著他們。

p.28-29 史帝沃跟安娜和伯爵夫人說了這件事情，他說：「太可怕了！他的妻子就在一旁，妻子往他的屍體撲過去，說她還有一大家子的人要養。好慘啊！」

「不能替她想點辦法嗎？」安娜的眼裡含著淚水問道。

馮斯基看了她一下，然後就走出車廂，過了幾分鐘後才又走回來，這時史帝沃正對著兩位女士在聊莫斯科最新的一齣戲劇。他們一起下了車廂，走向車站出口。當他走到車站門口時，站長從後面追了過來。

站長對馮斯基伯爵說：「這位先生，你給了副站長一大筆錢，您希望我們怎麼處理這筆錢？」

「喔，這當然是要給那位遺霜和他們的小孩。」馮斯基答道。

「你給他們錢？」史帝沃說：「你可真好心，真好心啊！」

隨後他們兩組人各自搭馬車返回住處。坐在返家的馬車上，安娜問道：「你和馮斯基先生認識很久了嗎？」

「是啊，你知道的，他想娶凱蒂。」

安娜一聽，心情整個大變。

「真的啊？」她輕聲說道：「現在談談你的事吧。」

p.30-31 史帝沃把一切都跟安娜說了。當他們抵家時，他讓安娜下車，自己就駕著馬車回縣府大樓上班。

朵麗嘴巴上雖然跟史帝沃說她不在乎安娜是不是要來，但當她見到安娜時，還是覺得很安慰。

「畢竟犯錯的又不是安娜，」她對自己說：「對我來說，她是一個親愛的朋友。」

當安娜一進門，朵麗熱切地迎接並親吻她。

「朵麗，能見到妳我好高興啊！」安娜說。

安娜很有同理心地傾聽著朵麗的談話，而朵麗能把自己的困擾說出來，心情也變得好多了。

「安娜，妳說我能怎麼辦？」朵麗在最後說道：「妳幫幫我吧。」

「朵麗，史帝沃的心還是在妳這裡的。」安娜說：「我是他妹，我知道他在想什麼。他只愛妳一個人——他心裡頭只有妳一個人。」

「如果他又偷腥了，」朵麗問：「妳能原諒他嗎？」

「我想他不會再偷腥了，」安娜答道，然後思索了一會兒，又說：「要是我，我會原諒他的。」

p.32-33 最後，朵麗接受了安娜的勸導，她原諒了史帝沃。就在朵麗答案原諒丈夫之後，凱蒂剛好來了。她是來找她的姐姐朵麗的。

凱蒂還沒正式見過安娜，但她知道安娜這個人。凱蒂希望這位聖彼得堡來的時尚女性，不會把她當成傻女孩來看。安娜很喜歡凱蒂，兩人相處融洽，這三位女士還閒聊了一個鐘頭左右。

凱蒂在離開之前，她跟安娜說：「妳下星期一定要來參加大舞會喔，那裡名流雲集！」

「妳的馮斯基伯爵也會到吧？」安娜問。

凱蒂一聽，臉都紅了。

「我今天在火車站很榮幸地遇到了他，」安娜說：「他長得很帥，而且很大方。我想我會留到下週的大舞會的。」

凱蒂離開之後，朵麗要僕人準備晚餐。當晚，朵麗、史帝沃、安娜和孩子們，大家齊聚晚餐。朵麗肯叫丈夫的名字了，她已經三天不叫他的名字了，所以這讓史帝沃很開心，也很感激安娜的幫忙。

p.34-35 席巴斯基的管家穿越市區，宣布雷文七點半會到。凱蒂聽到消息，心裡是既期待又怕受傷害。她很明白雷文要提早抵達的原因。

雷文走進大廳，看到凱蒂獨自一人站在那裡。他很興奮地看著她，可是卻一副靦腆的樣子。

「親愛的雷文！我聽說你回來莫斯科了！」凱蒂喊道：「你這次要待多久啊？」

「這就由妳決定了。」雷文說：「我是說，妳應該知道，我來是為了⋯⋯做我的妻子吧！」

凱蒂驚喜萬分。她很喜歡雷文，他們兩個人是青梅竹馬。只不過，她向來都把他當哥哥看，不太認為他會變成自己的老公。她沒想到，雷文的求婚竟會讓她這麼激動。但這時，她想到了馮斯基，所以她只是鎮靜地看著雷文。

「這是不可能的，」她輕聲說道：「原諒我吧。」

雷文靜靜地站了一會兒，然後傷心地說：「當然是不可能的，我懂。」

雷文要離開時，碰巧有一名英俊的男子穿著軍服走了進來。雷文看著凱蒂向馮斯基打招呼，凱蒂看馮斯基時，她的眼神和表情顯得神采飛揚。他看得出來，凱蒂真心愛著馮斯基。

p.36-37 下星期到來，莫斯科的大型宮殿舉行了一場盛大舞會。賓客們紛至沓來，舞會現場歡笑聲不絕於耳。凱蒂和她的母親稍後才以時髦之姿出現在舞會上。凱蒂身著一套黑色禮服，恰恰展現出她完美的身型。因此當她和母親步上台階時，眾人都以讚賞的眼光看著她。

隨後凱蒂就看到了舞會上最重要的人物們，正聚集在某個角落談話。史帝沃和朵麗就在那邊，身著黑色天鵝絨禮服的安娜也在那裡。安娜一點也不像是有個九歲兒子的婦女。而凱蒂的愛人馮斯基伯爵也在那個地方。一見到身穿帥氣制服的馮斯基，凱蒂心裡的小鹿就開始亂撞。

凱蒂加入了他們的談話，安娜讚美了凱蒂姣好的面貌。接著馮斯基便邀請凱蒂跳舞。他們只是閒話家常，不過凱蒂並不擔心，因為她確信馮斯基會邀請她跳晚會最重要的一支舞：馬祖卡舞曲。到時候他一定會向她求婚。

p.38-39 在第一支舞結束後，凱蒂又陸續和其他幾位男性共舞。這些男性競相要和她跳舞，她沒得選擇。然而就在她與其中一個男性跳舞時，凱蒂突然發現安娜正在一旁與馮斯基共舞。凱蒂變得有點擔心，因為他們兩個看起來很親密。安娜用明亮的雙眼看著馮斯基，每當馮斯基一開口說話，安娜就充滿喜

悅，眼神也更加閃爍。令凱蒂更恐懼的是，同樣的興奮與喜悅居然也出現在馮斯基的臉上。

最後一支舞曲馬祖卡開始了，就在她發現馮斯基已經和安娜跳起舞來，她接受了另一位男子的邀舞。這個男子是她們家的世交，叫做克隆斯基。凱蒂越看越覺得他們之間是彼此吸引，所以她的心受傷了。不久，安娜和凱蒂發現她們在彼此的旁邊跳舞，因此安娜把手伸向凱蒂，然而凱蒂視若無睹，而且還把手撥掉。此時安娜才發現了凱蒂臉上的絕望與嫉妒。

p.40-41 最後一首舞曲結束後，安娜告訴馮斯基說，她晚餐前就會離開。

「謝謝你給我這段美好的時光，」安娜說：「我現在得要走了，得去準備明天回去的行李。」

「所以你真的會明天離開是嗎？」馮斯基問道。

「我一定得走了。」安娜回答。她的明眸和微笑溫暖了馮斯基的心。

隔天早晨，安娜發了一封電報給丈夫，告知他，她會搭今晚的火車回聖彼得堡。

「我非走不可，」安娜對朵麗說：「我就跟你直說了，我之所以

突然要離開，是因為我破壞了凱蒂和馮斯基的好事。凱蒂很吃味，而且昨晚在舞會上，我讓她飽受煎熬。不過錯不在我，頂多，我只有一點點錯。」

「你現在好比是史帝沃一樣，」朵麗大聲說：「不過你一定要記得，安娜，我永遠都會把你當作是我最好的朋友。我不會忘記你為我所做的一切。」

當晚安娜搭上了回家的火車，這讓她感到舒坦、愉快多了。

「不久我就會看到親愛的兒子謝隆沙，還有我的丈夫了。」安娜對自己說道：「我的生活又可以恢復平靜了。」

## 第三章 愛在聖彼得堡

**p.44-45** 車外刮起了暴風雪，安娜想看看小說，卻無法專注。她聽著火車的聲音，漸漸睡著了。這時她發現，這班要前往聖彼得堡的火車突然停了下來。不久，一名身穿軍大衣的男子走近她。

「這位女士，有什麼需要我服務的嗎？」男子說道。

安娜從聲音認出了這名男子就是馮斯基。

「沒想到你也要去聖彼得堡。」安娜語帶喜悅地大聲說著：「你要去聖彼得堡做什麼？」

「你不猜猜看嗎？」馮斯基說道：「你到哪兒，我就跟去哪兒。」

安娜內心掙扎於喜悅與恐懼之間，她沈默了好一會兒後說道：「如果你是紳士就不該這麼說，我求你忘記，而且我也應該要忘記。」接著她閉上眼，想讓自己睡著。

隔天早上，卡列寧在火車站的月台等待妻子。就在安娜走下火車時，他們看見了對方。安娜一見到她的先生，那種熟悉的不悅感又浮現。對她來說，卡列寧冷酷，沒有情緒，也沒有熱情。

**p.46-47** 馮斯基走下火車，剛好看到卡列寧抓住安娜的樣子，那就好像她是他的財產一般。這是馮斯基第一次目睹到安娜是有男人的事實。他在看到卡列寧時，心中也產生了一種不愉快的感覺。馮斯基慢慢地走向卡列寧夫婦，說道：「昨晚睡得還好嗎？」

「睡得很好，謝謝。」安娜答道。她回答馮斯基的眼神是如此明亮。安娜看了看丈夫，想知道他是否認識馮斯基。卡列寧的臉上充滿不悅，他不喜歡被打擾，所以他想記住這個臭小子的樣子。

「這是馮斯基伯爵，」安娜說道：「我們在莫斯科認識的。」

「噢，我們之前見過面。」卡列寧面無表情地說道。

「希望改天能去拜訪你們。」馮斯基說道。「特別是安娜。」馮斯基內心想著。

「歡迎，我們每個星期一都會在家。」卡列寧用冷淡的語氣說道。

接著卡列寧轉身，手中仍舊抓著安娜，離開了車站。

p.48-49 安娜和丈夫回到家，他們的兒子謝隆沙看到了非常開心，他終於可以見到媽媽了。安娜告訴謝隆沙，她在莫斯科發生的事情，還給他帶了一些禮物。

在聖彼得堡，安娜常會和俄國的權貴們一起看歌劇、參加舞會。馮斯基伯爵的家族也是俄國的名門望族，他常會和安娜出現在同樣的場合裡。馮斯基是陸軍軍團的指揮官，他帶著部隊移防到聖彼得堡。

安娜回到聖彼得堡後，想要忘記和馮斯基的邂逅。然而每次在舞會上遇見馮斯基，又讓她感到興奮。不久安娜就意識到，和馮斯基在一起，已經成為她生活的重心了。安娜和馮斯基成為非常要好的知己，很多活動都聯袂出席。甚至當卡列寧太忙，無法陪安娜上戲院或是旅遊時，馮斯基都會陪她去。就這樣，他們兩人相戀了，這件事也成了俄國上流圈子的大八卦。卡列寧不是沒有注意到這件事，他也很在乎世俗的看法。不過他不是個莽撞的男人，所以他選擇不予理會。

p.50-51 這一天，馮斯基在卡列寧不在時去拜訪安娜。他在後陽台找到了安娜，她甜美的雙頰看起來又紅又熱。

「發生了什麼事？」馮斯基問道：「你生病了嗎？」

「不是，我懷孕了，」安娜答道：「是你的小孩。」

馮斯基聽了一臉慘白，用手扶住一旁的欄杆。

「我們要把事情作個了解，跟你丈夫提離婚吧，然後我們就可以結婚。」他説道。

「他不可能答應的，他不會讓我敗壞他們家族的門風。」安娜説。

「我們得跟他談，我們不能再這樣下去了。」馮斯基説道。

「那我們該怎麼做？」安娜問：「私奔嗎？」

馮斯基想了一下説道：「沒錯，這是唯一的辦法，他要是不肯離婚，我們就離開俄國。」

馮斯基並不了解，這對安娜來説有多麼困難。她愛馮斯基，但她也不想離開兒子。不過，她似乎沒得選擇。

p.52-53 當安娜告訴卡列寧，她愛上了馮斯基時，卡列寧很震驚。他一直不想去面對安娜和馮斯基的婚外情。如果安娜這樣的宣告，讓他不得不面對這個事實。

卡列寧將安娜送到莫斯科外的避暑別墅，因為他需要時間好好思考。

在一番精打細算後，卡列寧決定強迫安娜繼續留在他的身邊。

「我不會快樂，但她也好不到哪裡去。」卡列寧思量著：「所以這是最好的辦法。我不打算拋棄這個有罪的老婆，相反地，我要給她機會，讓她好好彌補過錯。」

卡列寧寫了一封信給安娜。

> 不論你過去的所作所為是好是壞，我認為我沒有權利去切斷上帝賦予我們的這段關係。這個家族不能因為我們其中一人的罪惡，就分崩離析。我們的生活要恢復成以前的樣子。我相信你為自己的行為感到懊悔，也不會再繼續錯下去。如果你回心轉意，我會確保你和你兒子未來無虞。希望你能儘速回到聖彼得堡。
>
> 卡列寧

p.54-55 安娜照丈夫所説的回到了聖彼得堡，她對現況感到很無助。

「我的人生還是跟以前一樣痛苦。現在卡列寧已經知道我不忠貞了，接下來怎麼辦？我肚子裡的小孩又該何去何從？」安娜心想。

安娜依舊和丈夫住在同一個屋子裡，他們一同共進晚餐，以免僕人閒言閒語。不過，安娜還是繼續在外頭和馮斯基幽會。卡列寧也知道，不過他只告訴安娜，決不能把他帶回家裡。

這一天，馮斯基收到安娜的紙條。

> 我好像生病了，病懨懨的。我沒辦法出去，可是我很想見你。請在十點前來找我。我的丈夫要開會，十點以前不會回到家。

馮斯基這時很累，他躺下來小憩片刻。他做了一個奇怪的夢，夢中有個佝僂的鄉下老粗，操著法文自言自語，他在夢裡受到了驚嚇。醒來後，他才發現只是一場夢。馮斯基看了看手錶，已經八點了，他得趕緊去看安娜才行。

p.56-57 馮斯基敲了安娜家的前門，來開門的僕人看到是馮斯基時，一臉驚訝。接著，換馮斯基露出驚訝的表情，因為他此時竟看見卡列寧走出門來。卡列寧停下腳步，用不悅的嚴峻眼神看了看馮斯基，然後坐上馬車，感覺就像是把馮斯基當成空氣一般。「如果他和我打架，我也許還可以有些反抗。」馮斯基想著：「但他卻讓我感覺自己好像個狡猾之人。」

馮斯基走進屋裡，發現安娜在大廳裡。

「為什麼你丈夫會在家？」馮斯基問道。

「他本來已經出門了，但突然有事回來。」安娜說：「很抱歉，讓你們互相撞見了。」

「你是生了什麼病？」馮斯基問道：「是因為你快生了嗎？」

安娜溫和地笑笑說：「我們的問題很快就會結束，我們就要得到解脫了。」

「什麼意思？」馮斯基問道。

「我會難產而死，」安娜說：「我昨晚夢見一個骯髒佝僂的鄉下老粗，他用法語不斷地喃喃自語。我很害怕，所以我想我會死於難產。」

馮斯基想起了他自己的夢，他一時之間也錯愕了。接著，他振作精神說道：「這些都是無稽之談，不會理會。」

p.58-59 隔天早晨，卡列寧沒敲門就走進安娜的房間。

卡列寧對安娜說：「我對你唯一的要求，就是不要把情夫帶進家裡，但你卻沒有做到。現在我要和你離婚，把兒子帶走。兒子會去和我妹妹一起住。」

安娜抓住卡列寧的手臂，叫道：「求求你，把謝隆沙留給我！」

卡列寧將她的手推開，走出房間。接下來的三天，他前去莫斯科出差。

在莫斯科，正當卡列寧和一名高級官員走在辦公室外時，有人叫住了他。他環顧四周，看到了安娜的哥哥歐隆斯基。卡列寧並不想見到他，但歐隆斯基跑過來和他說話。

「你怎麼沒告訴我你人在莫斯科？」歐隆斯基說道：「我們明晚要舉行一個宴會。你就在五、六點的時候蒞臨敝府吧。」

卡列寧猶豫了一下說道：「我沒辦法去，我沒有要冒犯的意思，只是，我要和你妹妹離婚了。」

歐隆斯基之前就有聽過他妹妹和卡列寧之間的傳言，他現在知道那不是開玩笑的，不過他一點也不想相信。他說：「不可能吧！安娜是一個很完美的女性。這其中一定有什麼誤會。」

「我也希望那真的只是誤會！」卡列寧答道。

### p.60-61

## 安娜：一個因緣際會的女主角

《安娜·卡列尼娜》不時被視為是史上最偉大的小說，然而諷刺的是，托爾斯泰當初卻是在偶然之下才創作出這個作品。當時托爾斯泰正在撰寫他的另一部小說《彼得大帝》，但他碰上了寫作的瓶頸。他處在沮喪的狀況下時，想起了友人 Bibikov 的故事。

Bibikov 和一位叫做 Anna Stepanova Pirogova 的女子同居。而托爾斯泰也就是借用這名女子的名字和他們之間所發生的悲劇，為這個故事塑型。Bibikov 離開 Anna，和一名對他的小孩照顧有加的德國家庭女教師結婚。Anna 得知消息後，就離開了。

Anna 帶著一包衣服，在鄉下待了三天。她寫了封信給 Bibikov，上面寫道：「你就是謀殺我的人，如果你覺得暗殺是件快樂的事，你就繼續高興下去吧。我的屍體會出現在亞先基火車站的軌道上。」接著，她躺在亞先基火車站的一節貨物車廂底下。

托爾斯泰隔天真的跑到亞先基火車站，在警方的監督下，現場觀看驗屍的情形。看著醫生檢驗 Anna 的屍體，托爾斯泰想像了這個可憐女子的生活。他考量了當時俄國上流社會，關於性、責任、婚姻和道德行為等議題。綜合這些思考後，他文思泉湧。

Leo Tolstoy (1828-1910)

## 第四章 寬恕與原諒

p.62-63 卡列寧回到孤單單的旅館後，看到了安娜打來的電報。

上頭寫著：

> 我快死了。我祈求你來一趟，因為你的原諒，能讓我死得安詳些。

「這該不會只是個把戲吧？可是如果她真的快要死了，而我卻不肯見她，這未免也太殘忍了。不行，我得回家一趟。」卡列寧說。

卡列寧知道，安娜不久就會生下馮斯基的孩子，他心安娜會這麼虛弱，是因為即將要臨盆了。

他一抵達門口，僕人隨即為他開門。

「夫人的情況怎麼樣了？」卡列寧問。

「她昨天生了一個女娃兒，她的身體會天還很虛，醫生們很擔心。」僕人答道。

卡列寧注意到走廊的牆上掛著陌生的帽子和外套。「現在還有誰在這裡？」他問道。

僕人猶豫了一下說：「先生，是馮斯基伯爵。」

p.64-65 卡列寧走上樓，看見馮斯基正坐在妻子的房門外。馮斯基用手埋住臉，接著他抬頭往上看，發現了卡列寧接近的腳步聲。

「她快死了，醫生都說沒希望了，就讓我待在這裡吧！」馮斯基說道。

卡列寧轉過身去，一句話都沒說就走進安娜的房間。安娜側躺著，用閃閃發亮的眼神正對著門。

「快過來，亞歷斯，」她說道：「我的時間不多了，病魔等會兒就會回來糾纏我，我就快死了。」

卡列寧跪在安娜的床邊，他把安娜的手放到自己的手心上，用另一隻手摸摸她的額頭。卡列寧可以感覺得到，在安娜蒼白的肌膚下，高燒就像熔爐般侵襲著她。

「再多留下來一會兒，亞歷斯，」安娜說道：「有些事我一定要告訴你，在我的身體裡有另一個女人，我很怕她，是她愛上了另一個男人的。我並不是那個女人，現在的我才是真正的我。我很清楚自己快死了，我只祈求你一件事，原諒我吧，請原諒我過去的一切。」

卡列寧的內心感受到一股愛、憐憫和寬恕，他將自己的頭埋進安娜的胸口。安娜胸口的高溫穿過衣服透出來，卡列寧忍不住哭了出來。

**p.66-67** 安娜看見馮斯基就站在門口。

「為什麼不讓他進來呢？」安娜問道：「快進來！快進來！亞歷斯，和他握手言和吧。」

馮斯基走進房間，站在安娜的床旁。

「和他握手吧，原諒他吧。」安娜對她的丈夫說。

卡列寧伸出他的右手示意，也不去理會自己臉上潛然淚下的淚珠。

「感謝老天爺！真的感謝老天爺！」安娜哭著說：「我的心願已了結，現在我可以安心地死去了，老天爺啊，這痛苦何時才會停止？」

不久醫生進門來，告訴卡列寧，所有像安娜這樣情況的病人，都不免一死，他並不認為她會活過今晚。然而，隔天早上安娜的情況並未惡化，所以醫生表示也許還有一絲希望。

卡列寧走進馮斯基待了一整晚的小房間，拿了把椅子，坐在情敵的面前。

「我之所以決定要離婚，是想懲罰她和你。」卡列寧說道：「我收到電報要趕回來時，內心的確五味雜陳。我承認我甚至希望她就這麼死去，但是當我看到她時，我就原諒她了。我的責任很簡單：我應

該，而且我也一定會陪著她。如果她想見你，我會通知你。不過我覺得你現在最好離開。」

**p.68-69** 馮斯基不解為何卡列寧可以如此冷靜與寬容，他就像一位紳士，體貼且令人可敬。比起自己，他要好得多了。從卡列寧家中返回自己的家時，馮斯基感到一股深深的慚愧、丟臉和罪惡感。

他根本無法入睡。事實上他最近才剛接到一個到烏茲別克的重要職務，不過一切都已經毫無意義了。安娜已經離開他了，而他的內心也充滿了無比的羞恥。

「我瘋了嗎？」他想了想：「這就是為什麼有些人會選擇自殺。」

馮斯基走到書桌前，拿出一把手槍。他對準自己的胸口，扣下扳機。馮斯基倒在地上，卻不覺得痛苦。他看見地毯上的血，意識到自己已經開槍了。

「蠢蛋！」他想：「我射偏了！」

接著眼前一片黑暗。他的僕人一聽到槍聲就跑進房間來。一看到這種情況，急忙跑去叫醫生。馮斯基躺在床上，儘管胸前有個大傷口，他的心臟卻依然強烈地在跳動著。

**p.70-71** 卡列寧已經完全原諒安娜了。當他知道馮斯基自殺未遂後，

145

他就更加地同情他。他也很憐憫謝隆沙這個兒子，雖然他對兒子不是太熱情。隨著時間過去，安娜逐漸康復了。卡列寧發現安娜很怕他，會盡量避著他。

安娜痊癒之後，就忘了當初對卡列寧說過的那些話。她只想去看看正從槍傷中復原的馮斯基，所以她每次想到丈夫時，都覺得自己罪孽深重。最後她決定派人去請哥哥歐隆斯基過來一趟。歐隆斯基一見到安娜，就對她說：「我知道很痛苦，但你必須振作。沒有什麼比你的幸福來得重要。」

「不，史帝沃，我已經迷失了，我的不幸還沒結束，而且結果會很悲慘。」安娜說道。

「你錯愛上一個不是你老公的男人，而你真正的丈夫卻原諒你了，但是，你可以和他繼續生活下去嗎？你想要這樣子嗎？他也想這樣維持下去嗎？」

「我不知道，我不知道他想要的是什麼。」安娜說。

「我來幫你解決這個問題。你們兩個都很悲慘！還有什麼更好的解決方法？離婚，就可以解決一切。我現在就去找他，把事情做個了斷。」歐隆斯基說。

p.72-73 歐隆斯基發現卡列寧坐在椅子上閱讀。

「希望我沒有打擾到你，」歐隆斯基進門時說道：「我想跟你談談我妹的事情。」

「我想應該也沒有什麼其他事可談，」卡列寧嘆了一口氣說：「看，我剛寫了封信要給她。」

卡列寧將信遞給歐隆斯基，上面寫道：

> 我知道你和我在一起並不快樂。我在你重病時承諾過，我會原諒你之前的一切。我唯一的希望，就是你再當回以前那個賢妻良母。不過現在看來不太可能了。告訴我該怎麼做，才能帶給你快樂與寧靜。只要你要求的，我都會允諾。

歐隆斯基驚訝地看著信，他對卡列寧的寬宏大量感到不可置信。

「我要知道她想要的是什麼。」卡列寧問道。

「這很簡單，她想要離婚。這樣一來，你們都能得到自由。」歐隆斯基回答。

「沒錯，如果她真的這麼希望，那我就放她走，就算她要帶走我兒子也沒關係。」卡列寧喊道。

歐隆斯基溫柔地笑著說：「相信我，她會感激你的所作所為，我只希望能盡可能幫助你們兩個人。」

## 第五章 嶄新的生活

p.76-77 馮斯基自殺後的幾天一直處於生與死的邊緣。他慢慢地康復了。當他的身體可以自由移動時，他決定放棄安娜。不過每每想起安娜，他心中仍有揮之不去的傷痛。當他從安娜的摯友貝特絲公主那裡得知卡列寧同意離婚時，便立刻去找安娜。馮斯基一點也不害怕碰到卡列寧，他就這樣前往安娜的房間、打開房門，把安娜緊緊地抱在懷裡。馮斯基在安娜的臉、脖子和肩膀上留下了無數的吻痕。

「我們一起去英國，把這裡的一切都拋下。」他告訴安娜。

安娜顫抖著，內心交雜著興奮與恐懼。
「我們真的可以像一般夫妻那樣的生活嗎？」她問道：「史帝沃告訴我，他同意離婚，但他肯放棄謝隆沙嗎？」

「現在別擔心這些，別去想它。」馮斯基說道。

「但願我當時就死了，也許那樣會好過一點，」安娜淚潸潸地說道：「不過能再次看見你，我還是非常高興。」

p.78-79 馮斯基從沒想過自己會那麼快從軍中退下。不過做出決定的那一天，他沒有任何的遲疑。他花了一個禮拜的時間安排安娜和他們的女兒離開聖彼得堡。他們前往義大利，並且認為卡列寧會趁他們不在時辦好離婚手續。

馮斯基和安娜花了三個月的時間在歐洲旅遊，最後在義大利的一個小鎮買了一棟不大的房子，在那裡定居了三個月。安娜此生從沒這麼快樂過，她的身體完全都康復了。她越了解馮斯基，對他的愛就越深。安娜最後終於獨佔馮斯基，他的存在就是她活力的來源。安娜完全將丈夫和兒子的事情拋諸腦後。她越來越寵愛女兒安，這三個月來，她幾乎都忘了謝隆沙。

馮斯基對於能夠離開軍隊和原本的社交圈，也同樣感到愉快。剛開始的日子的確很幸福，不過幾週後，他就開始不耐煩了。他沒有工作、沒有職責來填充每一天的時間。於是他們決定搬到馮斯基家族在聖彼得堡附近的莊園。不過首先安娜要先在聖彼得堡停留一陣子，因為她想看看她的兒子。

p.80-81 安娜離開後，卡列寧變得很沮喪。他不了解，為什麼在放安娜和姦夫走之後，他會那麼孤獨。而且每次出門，都讓他覺得很丟臉，因為他知道人人都在討論、嘲笑他。

安娜離開後的幾天，卡列寧收到了一張帽子店寄來的帳單。這筆安娜的未付帳款，讓他深感失落，讓他難過得坐下來大哭。

麗迪雅伯爵夫人是一名虔誠的女性，她很年輕就結婚了，不過丈夫卻在兩個月後與她離異。麗迪雅對卡列寧頗有好感，因此當她得知安娜棄卡列寧而去時，她更加不捨卡列寧這個可憐人。麗迪雅決定去拜訪卡列寧，而此時他正躲在書房裡暗泣。麗迪雅發現卡列寧正用雙手抱著頭，感覺非常懊惱。

「我什麼事都聽說了！」麗迪雅握著卡列寧的手，說道：「我親愛的朋友，我知道你很難過，但你要變得更堅強啊！」

p.82-83 卡列寧熱淚盈眶地看著麗迪雅，說道：「最令我難過的，不是失落感，而是我覺得很丟人現眼！還有，我發現自己整天都在處理家務事，我要吩咐僕人、照顧小孩，還要忙著付帳單。」

「這我都懂，親愛的朋友。」麗迪雅說道：「你需要一位女性幫忙你處理這些家務事，你可以相信我，我可以幫你打理好一切。」

卡列寧用感激的表情，靜靜地握住麗迪雅的手。

「我會幫你處理家務事，然後我們可以一起照顧謝隆沙。」麗迪雅說道：「不用對我表示感謝，要感謝就感謝上帝吧！只有祂才能讓我們找到寧靜、舒適和關愛。」

「真的很謝謝你。」卡列寧說。

麗迪雅笑著拍拍他的背，然後去找謝隆沙，抱一抱他。她告訴他，他的父親是個聖人，而他的母親已經死了。

當麗迪雅得知安娜和馮斯基回到聖彼得堡時，她很恐慌。她想，自己一定要保護卡列寧，不可以讓他再看見這個骯髒的女人，所以麗迪雅決定不讓卡列寧知道這件事。

p.84-85 隔天，麗迪雅收到安娜的來信，上頭寫道：

親愛的伯爵夫人：

和兒子分開，真的讓我很難過。所以在離開聖彼得堡之前，我一定要再見他一面。我會寫信給你，是因為卡列寧見到我一定會很難過，我不想造成他的負擔。我知道你和他的關係不錯，所以你一定可以諒解我的行為。不知道你可否帶謝隆沙來看我，不然我在卡列寧不在家時，過去造訪也可以。非常感謝你的幫助。

安娜

148

麗迪雅對於安娜的來信感到不悅，所以她決定不顧安娜的顧慮，把這件事告訴卡列寧。

卡列寧一回到家，麗迪雅就把安娜的信拿給他看。卡列寧仔細地閱讀後説道：「我不認為我有權利拒絕她。」

「我親愛的朋友，你把每個人都看得太好了。」麗迪雅大聲説。

「我已經原諒她了，我不能阻止她對兒子付出關心。」卡列寧回答。

「但你確定她是真心的嗎？」麗迪雅問：「她對愛是忠誠的嗎？我們可以讓她這樣隨意玩弄小孩的感情嗎？他認為她已經死了，甚至為她禱告。假如謝隆沙看到母親，他會有多驚訝！」

「我沒想這麼多。」卡列寧説。

「如果你接受我的建議，就拒絕她來看兒子的要求吧。你贊同的話，我這就去回覆她。」麗迪雅説。

p.86-87 卡列寧勉強答應了她的提議，麗迪雅伯爵夫人馬上寫了一封信給安娜：

太太：

讓你的兒子看見你，可能會引起他的諸多疑惑，而這也不是三言兩語就能解釋清楚的問題。所以你們最好別見面，願上帝憐憫你。

麗迪雅伯爵夫人

安娜被這封信一激，決定隔天就去看兒子，這天碰巧也是兒子的生日。安娜早上跑去看謝隆沙，因為她知道這時他正在睡覺。應門的僕人看到安娜時，很是吃驚，不發一語。安娜馬上前往兒子的房間，看到他正在睡覺。

「謝隆沙！」安娜輕聲地説道。她內心想著兒子都長那麼大了，他現在變得又高又瘦。

不過他還是原本那個謝隆沙，她最深愛的兒子。謝隆沙動一動身體、擺擺頭，就好像他正在作夢一般。他張開雙眼，遲疑地看了母親好幾秒，接著他突然露出潔白的牙齒，迸出大大的微笑。謝隆沙滿意地投入母親的懷抱。

p.88-89 「謝隆沙，我最親愛的小寶貝！」安娜説道。

「媽咪！我就知道你會來，我就是知道。現在我要快點起床囉……」他説道。

安娜看著他，不禁流下淚來。

「你不認為我已經死了嗎？」安娜問道。

「我根本就不相信！我知道你會來！」謝隆沙説道。接著他笑著說：「媽咪！你坐到我的衣服了。」

「謝隆沙，你一定要敬愛你的父親，他是一個比我更好更棒的人。我之前對他太壞了。等你長大了，你就會理解。」安娜說。

「沒有人可以取代你。」謝隆沙哭著說。

突然間，卡列寧把門打開，走了進來，他看到安娜時楞了一下，不過卻面無表情。謝隆沙坐了起來，開始嚎啕大哭。安娜親了親他那被淚水弄濕的臉龐，起身準備要走。卡列寧閃到一邊方便讓安娜通過，並對她點頭示意。

## p.90-91 19世紀的俄國女人

身為19世紀的俄國女人，不論幸與不幸，皆身處於弱勢的地位。就算是像安娜‧卡列尼娜這樣的貴族女性，都無法在政治上謀得一官一職。她們無法擁有護照，不能上中學或是大學。俄國女性唯一的目標就是嫁人，而且要嫁得好。夫妻雙方的家世背景要門當戶對，鮮有自由戀愛。

婚後的女人，總是背負相夫教子的期待，而且丈夫掌控了妻子的一切大小事務。俄國婦女的一切都被規定在嚴苛的行為準則內，社會規定婦女結婚前一定要是處女。服從，是婚後女性的最高美德，違反者會得到嚴厲的處分，她們將會受到暴力對待，或是被驅逐出這個社會。

在托爾斯泰的這個年代，俄國的知識份子開始關切到這個社會體系的不公。有趣的是，其實托爾斯泰剛開始將安娜設定為一個醜陋且邪惡的角色，後來才改成現在這樣。如此人們才會對安娜加以同情，並且開始去質疑這個偽善的體系：它可以如此嚴苛地懲罰犯錯的女性，但對於犯相同錯誤的男人，卻可以視若無睹。

## 第六章 最後的嫉妒

p.92-93 從卡列寧的住處返回旅館後，安娜失控大哭。

「為什麼在我最需要馮斯基的時候，他卻不在我身邊？」安娜思考著。她開始絕望地想著馮斯基也已經離她遠去。「我已經完全被這個世界給遺棄了。」她哭著說。

安娜趕快請飯店人服務人員捎了一封信給馮斯基，詢問他是否可以馬上回來。不久，服務人員收到馮斯基的回信，上頭表示他很快就會和朋友亞信王子一起回來。

安娜的內心冒出一種奇怪的想法：「他怎麼不是自己回來，如果他不是一個人，我要怎麼和他傾訴我現在的痛苦感受。他真的還愛我嗎？他是不是想避開和我獨處？如果真的不愛我了，就該和我講清楚才對。」

雖然安娜的內心感到不安，但馮斯基和亞信出現時，她還是展現出一貫的迷人之姿。他們三人一起共進晚餐時，亞信滔滔不絕地談論政治，而馮斯基也聽得津津有味。安娜很強烈地受到，馮斯基想前往莫斯科競選公職。

p.94-95 亞信離開後，安娜說：「如果能住在你那位於鄉下的莊園，那就太好了。」

馮斯基猶豫了一下，面露慚色。

「事實上，我母親最近住在那裡。」馮斯基回答：「現在過去那裡住可能不太好，而且我們還在等待你的離婚手續。」

安娜感到非常迷惘。在接下來的幾天，馮斯基都會獨自前往晚宴或是歌劇院。安娜不能同行，因為她一定會成為大家八卦的主角。馮斯基決定要成為一名政治家，所以他會參加這些場合藉以攀關係。在這段期間，安娜很吃味，她不斷在想像馮斯基接觸了多少的年輕女性。她很害怕他會愛上其他女人，這是最讓她害怕的事，因為馮斯基曾不假思索地告訴她，他的母親希望他能娶年輕的索羅金娜公主。

p.96-97 這天晚上，安娜突然厭倦獨自待在家裡，所以她自己跑去看歌劇。演出時，有一個坐在旁邊的皇室成員向她打招呼，他們是舊識，然而他的老婆卻突然站起來，說從來沒有看過像安娜這麼不要臉的女人。接著他的老婆轉身離開，他自己也尾隨而去。這名皇室成員唯一能做的，就是向安娜點頭表示同情。大部分在場的觀眾都目睹了這件事情。安娜感到無比的羞恥，整個人結凍似的坐在椅子上。

幾分鐘後，她返回旅館開始痛哭。

p.98-99 安娜正在等馮斯基從晚宴回來，他們前一天才剛吵過架，而且馮斯基也因此整天都不在家。安娜感到悲慘和孤獨，所以她決定原諒馮斯基，和他和好如初。

當馮斯基到家時，她說道：「親愛的，玩得還愉快嗎？」

馮斯基看安娜心情還不錯，所以答道：「不錯啊！」

「親愛的，我今天坐車出去透氣，感覺真好，這讓我想起了鄉下，你媽已經搬回莫斯科，你的家族莊園已經沒人住了。」安娜說。

「沒錯，那你認為我們何時要搬過去？」馮斯基說。

「後天怎麼樣？」安娜建議。

「可以啊，噢！不對，那天不行。」馮斯基說道：「後天是星期日，我要去看我媽。」

馮斯基覺得有點心虛，因為安娜用狐疑的眼神看著他。

p.100-101 「我們明天就可以搬過去。」安娜說道。

「不行，我找我媽是因為有正事要辦。明天不可能。」

「既然這樣，那就不要搬過去算了。」安娜說。

「為什麼這樣說？」馮斯基驚訝地問道：「我們可以幾天之後再搬過去！」

「不用了，」安娜說道：「如果你還愛我，你一定會想馬上就搬過去。如果你的心已經不在我身上了，那我們之間就到此為止吧！」

安娜作勢要離開，馮斯基抓住了她的手。

「等等，我現在一頭霧水，我只是說要延個幾天而已，你卻責怪我不再愛你了。」他說道。

安娜看都不看馮斯基一眼，甩開他手，走出了房間。

「很明顯地，他討厭我！」安娜心想：「他一定是愛上別人了。」

想到生產時的痛楚，她恨不得自己當時就死了。

「如果我死了，那麼現在帶給我先生和兒子的恥辱，都會煙消雲散。」她想著：「如果我死了，他也會因此內疚不已。」

p.102-103 隔天早上，安娜和馮斯基共進早餐時，來了一封給馮斯基的電報。他讀了電報，似乎不想讓安娜看到內容。安娜問他電報是誰捎的。

「是史帝沃。」他說道。

「那為什麼不給我看？」安娜問道。

「好吧！好吧！」馮斯基不甘願

地答道：「你自己看吧！」

電報上頭寫著：

> 我見過卡列寧了，離婚的希望非常渺茫。

安娜說道：「這何必隱瞞我？這對我來說一點都不重要。你這麼在意幹嘛？」

馮斯基感到沮喪。他說：「我喜歡一切都很明確，而我認為你會生氣，是因為你的立場不夠堅定。」

「我的立場堅定得很，」安娜答道：「我完全在你的掌握之中，明明就是你的立場不夠明確！」

「安娜，如果你認為我想要自由……」馮斯基想解釋。

安娜打斷了他的話，說道：「我根本不在意你媽怎麼想，或是她希望你娶誰。」

p.104-105 「這根本就是兩回事！」馮斯基吼道。

「是同一回事，」安娜答道：「讓我來告訴你吧，我一點也不在意你那個冷酷的母親，我一點也不想和她牽扯上關係。」

馮斯基變得冷酷而憤怒。「我不准你這麼說我母親，放尊重點！」

\* \* \*

安娜一整天都把自己關在房間裡。她突然又想起，死亡是解決目前窘境的唯一方法。一切都已經無所謂了——不管搬到鄉下與否。最重要的，是要好好懲罰馮斯基這個人。安娜躺下來睡個午覺，再次夢到操著法語喃喃自語的佝僂老粗。

她突然嚇醒，聽見外頭的馬車聲。安娜看見窗外有一位年輕的妙齡女子從馬車內探出身來，馮斯基隨即跑出門外，從女子手上接了一個包裹。他對女子說了一些話，她也予以微笑回應。等馬車走遠了，馮斯基才回到屋內。

p.106-107 安娜因恐懼和憤怒而顫抖，她往馮斯基的書房走去，決定告訴他，她要和他分開。

「那就是索羅金娜公主，她幫我媽送來一些文件。明天我們就一起去拜訪她好嗎？」馮斯基說。

「你自己去吧，我不會跟你走的，」安娜說道，作勢要離開。

「安娜，我們不能再繼續這樣下去……」

「你會為此感到懊悔的。」安娜說畢即離開。

馮斯基從安娜的眼神中看到了沮喪，他本來要起身去追她，最後卻坐了下來。

「算了，我已經盡力了，她現在需要的是獨處。」他心想。

他派人叫了馬車，準備起程前往

母親的住處。馬車不久就到了，馮斯基搭上馬車，離開了旅館。

安娜從窗戶內看到馮斯基離去，一股莫名的恐懼緊緊地揪住她的心。

「他真的棄我而去了！一切都結束了！」她心想著。

安娜衝下樓去，問僕人說馮斯基是去哪裡。

僕人答道：「火車站，他要搭火車前往歐碧洛佳。」

p.108-109 歐碧洛佳是馮斯基母親的居所住的地區。安娜坐下來，寫了一張便條：

都是我的錯，快回來吧！我們需要談談。看在上帝的份上，回來吧。我真的很害怕。

僕人帶著便條離去，半個小時後返回並告訴安娜說，他到火車站時，馮斯基已經搭車離去了。安娜趕緊寫了一封電報，請僕人捎過去，上頭寫著：

我們一定得現在談談，請馬上回來。

「我現在就搭車過去和他談談。」安娜心想。

她看了看火車時刻表，找到了下一班前往歐碧洛佳的車是一個小時後。安娜派人叫了馬車，前往車站。一路上，安娜看到了街上來來往往的行人，他們的生活對她來說毫無意義。一到火車站，馬車夫問安娜：「我要幫你買前往歐碧洛佳的車票嗎？」

「要。」安娜答道。她看了看其他正在等車的人，沒有一個人讓她看順眼的。

p.110-111 當安娜拿到車票，坐上火車，她覺得車上的人都以一種奇怪且不友善的眼神看著她。安娜往窗戶外面看了看，發現有名骯髒的老人正彎著腰，看著火車輪。

「這個場景有點熟悉。」安娜想著。不久，火車開動了。當安娜抵達了歐碧洛佳，下車後她馬上問電報的工作人員，有沒有馮斯基伯爵捎來的訊息。

「有的，女士，我剛剛才拿到，在這裡。事實上馮斯基伯爵的馬車夫，剛剛才從這裡載走了索羅金娜公主。」工作人員回答。

安娜看了馮斯基情急之下寫的電報，上頭寫著：

我剛剛才收到你的電報，我十點才會回去。

「這就對了，正如我所料！」安

155

娜想著。她想像，如果自己走進馮斯基母親的家裡，看見索羅金娜公主在那裡，自己會有多麼丟臉。

「那麼，我該何去何從？」她一個人獨自徘徊在月台時思考著。安娜想要獨處，恰巧月台尾端剛好沒半個人。整個月台隨著另一班火車的接近而躁動起來。

p.112-113 此時安娜突然想起第一次遇見馮斯基那天，臥軌自殺的那個人。現在她知道自己該做什麼，安娜走下台階，往軌道的方向走去，看著即將進站的火車車輪。

「就是那個地方，就在車輪與車輪之間，我要跪在那裡，懲罰那個男人，然後此從這卑微的人生中解脫。」她想著。

安娜錯過了第一班車，不過第二班車來時，她馬上跪了下來。就在車廂的車輪經過時，安娜身子向前跪到鐵軌上。這時，她對於自己此時的行為感到非常恐懼。

「我在哪裡？我在做什麼？我為什麼要這樣做？」她突然這樣想著。

安娜想起身後退，但突然有個巨大的東西撞到她的後腦杓、拖著她，把她的身體整個往下壓。

「上帝啊，原諒我的所作所為吧！」她這樣想著。當時有名髒兮兮的老粗正在軌道的另一邊工作著，他喃喃自語，沒有注意到安娜正被火車沿著鐵軌輾下去。安娜眼前出現了過去的種種：她所有的謊言、悲傷和邪惡，一切的一切，在這一瞬間都變得非常明亮。這是她第一次清楚看見隱藏在自己心中的所有黑暗面。隨後，這道光突然變暗，消失不見。

Adaptor

Brian J. Stuart

University of Birmingham (MA – TESL/TEFL)
Sungshin Women's University, English Professor


Grade 5 **Anna Karenina**
Reprinted December, 2014

Original Author: Lev Nikolaevich Tolstoy
Adaptor: Brian J. Stuart
Illustrator: Nika Tchaikovskaya

Printed and distributed by Cosmos Culture Ltd.
Tel: 02-2365-9739
Fax: 02-2365-9835
http://www.icosmos.com.tw
Email: onlineservice@icosmos.com.tw

Let's Enjoy Masterpieces!—Anna Karenina
Copyright©2005 Darakwon Publishing Company
First published by Darakwon Publishing Company, Seoul, Korea
Taiwanese Translation Copyright@Cosmos Culture Ltd. 2010